"I love the way this man writes! I adore his style. There is something about it that makes me feel as if I'm someplace I'm not supposed to be, seeing things I'm not supposed to see and that is so delicious."
REBECCA FORESTER, USA Today Bestselling Author

This book "is creative and captivating. It features bold characters, witty dialogue, exotic locations, and non-stop action. The pacing is spot-on, a solid combination of intrigue, suspense, and eroticism. A first-rate thriller, this book is damnably hard to put down. It's a tremendous read."
FOREWORD REVIEWS

"A terrifying, gripping cross between James Patterson and John Grisham. Jagger has created a truly killer thriller."
J.A. KONRATH, USA Today and Amazon Bestselling Author

"As engaging as the debut, this exciting blend of police procedural and legal thriller recalls the early works of Scott Turow and Lisa Scottoline."
LIBRARY JOURNAL

"The well-crafted storyline makes this a worthwhile read. Stuffed with gratuitous sex and over-the-top violence, this novel has a riveting plot."
KIRKUS REVIEWS

"Verdict: The pacing is relentless in this debut, a hard-boiled novel with a shocking ending. The supershort chapters will please those who enjoy a James Patterson–style page-turner"

A "clever and engrossing mystery tale involving gorgeous women, lustful men and scintillating suspense."
FOREWORD MAGAZINE

"Part of what makes this thriller thrilling is that you sense there to be connections among all the various subplots; the anticipation of their coming together keeps the pages turning."
BOOKLIST

"This is one of the best thrillers I've read yet."
New Mystery Reader Magazine

"A superb thriller and an exceptional read."
MIDWEST BOOK REVIEW

"Verdict: This fast-paced book offers fans of commercial thrillers a twisty, action-packed thrill ride."
LIBRARY JOURNAL

"Another masterpiece of action and suspense."
NEW MYSTERY READER MAGAZINE

"Fast paced and well plotted . . . While comparisons will be made with Turow, Grisham and Connelly, Jagger is a new voice on the legal/thriller scene. I recommend you check out this debut book, but be warned . . . you are not going to be able to put it down."
CRIME SPREE MAGAZINE

"A chilling story well told. The pace never slows in this noir

thriller, taking readers on a stark trail of fear."
CAROLYN G. HART, N.Y. Times and USA Today Bestselling
Author

KILL ME FRIDAY

Thriller Publishing Group, Inc.

KILL ME FRIDAY

R.J. JAGGER

Thriller Publishing Group, Inc.

KILL ME FRIDAY

Thriller Publishing Group, Inc.
Golden, Colorado 80401

Copyright©RJJagger

Library of Congress Control Number: Available

ISBN 978-1-937888-85-5 (Hardcover)

Cover image by Robert A. Maguire
Used with permission

For Eileen

DAY ONE

July 15
Tuesday

1

Day One
July 15
Tuesday Morning

As soon as the woman walked through the office door, private investigator Bryson Wilde felt his world shift ever so slightly. Men would crawl across a field of broken glass just to smell her neck, that's the kind of woman she was--long strawberry hair, lips as hot as Havana asphalt, green eyes, a curvy squeeze-me body, a tight little waist cinched in a black belt, nylons that rustled like bedroom chimes, a scent like Paris, mid-twenties, expensive on every level.

Wilde tried to appear unaffected as the woman took one last drag from a cigarette, mashed the butt in the ashtray, slipped into one of the worn leather chairs in front of his desk and crossed her legs.

"You're Bryson Wilde," she said. "If I talk to you about a matter, is it strictly confidential?"

"Whatever you tell me, I take it to the grave."

She studied him.

"I'm not looking for 99 percent confidential," she said. "I'm looking for a hundred. If that's not you, if you got loose lips, if you get drunk and tell stories, then tell me now and save us both the time."

"Every client gets a hundred percent confidentiality," he said. "That's my promise."

She studied him, looking for lies or exaggerations.

She must not have found any because she pulled an envelope from her purse and pushed it across the desk. It was thick. Even if it was stuffed only with ones, there was still a chunk of change.

"That's three hundred dollars," she said.

Three hundred dollars.

A month's pay.

The corner of his mouth wanted to turn up ever so slightly, but he fought to keep it down and said, "So what can I do for you, exactly, Miss—"

"Neva."

Neva.

Nice.

"Do you have a last name, Neva?"

"I do but it's not important," she said. "A woman was murdered Saturday night. A woman named Grace Somerfield. Have you heard about her?"

He had.

Everyone had.

Grace Somerfield was a high-society socialite, a well-liked woman of prominence and presence. Divorced from high-profile attorney Everett Somerfield last year, she now lived alone in a stately mansion on Capitol Hill. Someone broke in Saturday night and robbed her. Before leaving, he slit her throat from ear to ear.

"What about her?" Wilde asked.

"I know who killed her," Neva said.

"Well that's interesting."

"Isn't it?"

Wilde pulled a book of matches out of his shirt pocket, peeled off a solitary stick and struck it, bringing the pungent odor of sulfur into the air. He used the fire to ignite the whole pack and let the flames twitch in his fingers for a few seconds before throwing them into the ashtray.

"So who killed Grace Somerfield?"

Neva collected her thoughts.

"Okay," she said. "Saturday night, after dark, I was in a car with a woman. We were parked on a side street up on Capitol Hill. It was storming out pretty hard."

"I remember," Wilde said. "It started about ten."

"Right," she said. "What I'm telling you about happened around ten-thirty or eleven. Anyway, me and the woman were in the backseat getting friendly, if you catch my drift."

"How friendly?"

"Very."

"You're a lesbian?"

"I am but I don't discriminate," she said.

"So what does that mean, you're bi?"

"Bi, tri, wherever the mood takes me," she said. "The point is, my friend was on her back. I was on top, straddling her face, meaning my head was up and I could see out the window. A woman came running out of the back yard of a mansion across the street. She headed for the car that was parked directly in front of ours. I lowered my head so she wouldn't see me. She got in her car, fired it up and squealed out. The whole thing was so weird that I looked at her license plate as she took off. It was FC211."

"Okay," Wilde said.

"That was pretty much the end of it until Monday when I saw in the paper that a rich woman named Grace Somerfield got murdered in her Capitol Hill house Saturday night," she said. "I went back there and looked around. It turns out that the woman I saw running Saturday night was coming from the address that belonged to Grace Somerfield."

"Interesting," Wilde said.

Neva nodded, pulled a cigarette out of her purse, dangled it in her mouth and gave one to Wilde. He lit them up and said, "Did you get a look at her face?"

She blew smoke.

"I got a fairly good look," she said. "She was young, I'd guess about my age and very pretty. Her hair was blond. She had it pulled up into a ball. There was a tattoo behind her ear. It wouldn't have shown if she had her hair down but, like I said, it was up."

"A tattoo?"

"Right, something black, right here," she said, pointing.

"What was it?"

She shrugged.

"I don't know," she said. "It was about the size of a quarter and either black or dark blue. I didn't see any reds or yellows or anything colorful like that."

"Could it have been a birth mark?"

"No, it was a tattoo. She was carrying a black bag. It looked like one of those bags doctors use."

Wilde stood up, walked over to the window and pulled it up. No air came in, no air went out, no air moved anywhere. Down below, Larimer Street buzzed.

"I don't get why you're telling me this," he said.

"Here's my dilemma. The woman I was with Saturday night can't be associated with any of this. She has a reputation to maintain. She won't have anything to do with filing a report. She's also made it clear that I'm not supposed to file one either. She wants both of us totally, one hundred percent, uninvolved. She says the police will eventually figure it out without any help."

"Who is this woman?"

"That's not important."

She took a long drag on the cigarette, mashed it in the ashtray hardly smoked and stood up.

"What I want you to do is be me Saturday night," she said. "Pretend you were in the area taking a walk or something—say you were taking shelter from the storm next to a tree, something like that—and make a police report. All you have to do is give them the information I just gave you."

"You want me to be a fake witness?"

Neva frowned.

"*Fake* isn't the right word," she said. "Fake implies there was no witness at all. *Substitute's* a better word. You'd be a substitute witness."

Wilde pictured it.

Then he shook his head and braced himself to say something he didn't want to say.

"I'm sorry, I really am, but that's not the kind of thing I do."

Neva wrinkled her forehead but didn't pick up the envelope. Instead she walked to the door, stopped halfway through, turned and said, "Then find someone who does. Justice is calling. Answer it."

Then she left.

Wilde watched her from the window as she swaggered down to 16th Street and disappeared behind an ice truck. He turned on the radio and twisted the dial until he got a song he liked, "Rocket 88." While Jackie Brenston filled the speakers with the virtues of his Buick, Wilde circled the desk three times, staring at the envelope, then picked it up and counted what was inside.

It was all there.

Three hundred singles.

He slipped it into the top drawer.

Something was wrong.

What?

He couldn't figure it out.

He was 31 years old and wore his hair combed straight back. It was blond, thick, longer than most and played well against his green eyes and Colorado tan. He wore his usual attire, namely a grey suit, a white long-sleeve shirt rolled up at the cuffs, a loose blue tie and spit-shinned wingtips. His hat, ashen-grey, was over on the rack. When he went out it would go on, dipped over his left eye. With a strong body topping out at six-two, he was every bit Neva's equal.

Suddenly he figured out what was wrong.

His gun was supposed to be in the drawer.

It wasn't there when he put the envelope in.

What the hell?

Suddenly he heard a crashing noise from the other part of his office, the room behind the adjoining door.

Someone was in there.

He took a deep breath and headed that way.

A man had his back against the wall, facing straight ahead, when Wilde came into the room. He was smaller, in fact considerably smaller, but he had the gun in hand. With a cat-quick move, he raised the weapon and pointed it at Wilde's chest.

Wilde froze.

Four steps away.

That's how far he was.

Four steps.

Four eternities.

Too far.

He lunged.

The gun exploded before his feet even left the ground.

2

Day One
July 15
Tuesday Morning

The bullet didn't stop Wilde. It may have hurt him, maybe even mortally, but it didn't kill him on the spot and that's all he needed to close the gap and swing a furious fist at the shooter's face. His knuckles connected solidly. Wham! The man's head snapped back and his body dropped to the floor and slammed face down. Wilde stood over him with a cocked arm, ready to explode on the back of his head if it moved even an inch.

No movement came.

Not an iota.

Wilde straightened up, nudged the body with his foot and got no response.

Was he dead?

Wilde didn't care.

Screw him.

It was self-defense.

He looked down at his chest for blood and found none. Same for his arms. Where did the bullet get him? He darted into the bathroom and checked his face in the mirror. There was no blood, not a drop, not anywhere.

He hadn't been hit.

How could anyone miss that close?

He walked back to the body, rolled it face up and pulled the man's hat off. Something unexpected happened, namely a good amount of light brown hair escaped from under it. Closer examination of the man's face showed he wasn't a man at all.

He was a woman.

Her face had no makeup.

She appeared to be in her mid-twenties.

The right side of her face was swelling up and beginning to turn a strange color. Wilde felt her pulse and got one. Then, just to be sure, he put his ear by her mouth and heard breathing.

Okay.

She wasn't dead.

He checked the wall to see how close the bullet came to hitting him. Naturally, it wasn't showing up, because that's the way his life worked. It should be easy to find. Where the hell was it?

Then he saw it.

It wasn't in the wall at all.

It was in the ceiling.

Straight above the woman's body.

Wilde slumped to the floor and studied her. So, she hadn't tried to kill him after all. She'd merely fired a warning shot.

Wilde smiled.

That was pretty gutsy.

Pretty gutsy indeed.

More gutsy than he would have been if someone twice his size was charging.

At the woman's feet was a pillowcase filled with odds and ends from the office. Wilde put everything back where it belonged, including the gun, and thought about calling the police before deciding against it. Instead he went back to the desk and re-counted the three hundred dollars again, coming up with 299 this time.

Two minutes later he heard the shower running.

Wilde pulled a clean white shirt out of the coat closet, opened the bathroom door just enough to reach through and hang it on the inside knob, then went back into the main room and stared out the window.

His office was in the 1600 block of Larimer Street, on the second floor above the Ginn Mill and two doors down from the Gold Nugget Tap Room. Right outside his building was a water fountain sculpture with cherubs, a throwback to the area's better days.

The water didn't run anymore.

Once the retail heart of Denver, now Larimer Street and its backdoor cousin, Market Street, were an unhealthy mixture of liquor stores, bars, gambling houses, brothels and flophouses, occasionally punctuated with the sound of gunplay. If this section of Denver was a smoke it wouldn't be a Camel or a Marlboro, it would be a cigar—not the worst cigar in the world, not the one that creeps into everything it touches and dies an immediate stinky death, but a cigar nevertheless.

Wilde didn't care.

He could afford an office in a nicer section of town, say over on 16th Street near the Daniels & Fisher Tower, or even over on 17th Street near the Brown Palace, but he wasn't inter-ested. He liked it fine right here, smack dab in the middle of the universe, and didn't apologize for his taste.

He liked the buzz.

He liked the edginess.

He especially liked the nights. That's when the dames got dangerous, cigarettes dangled from ruby-red lips and the tension got steamier than a Norma Jeane Mortenson movie down at the Zaza Theater. That's when whiskey-soaked jazz weaved out of apartment windows and the headlights of Packards and Hudsons and Studebakers and Buicks and Fords and Chevys punched up and down the asphalt.

The shower shut off.

Five minutes later, the woman came through the door, barefoot and barelegged, wearing the shirt. Her hair was flat and dripping with water, but she scrubbed up pretty nice. She looked to be about twenty-three or twenty-four. Her eyes showed that life had dealt her a few blows and there were more to come. The left side of her face was in bad shape, thanks to Wilde's fist.

"I figured if I'm going to jail, I'm at least going clean," she said.

"You're not going to jail," Wilde said. "You can leave."

"I don't understand."

He shook his head.

Then he did something he didn't expect; he pulled the envelope out of the drawer and tossed it to her.

"Take this with you," he said.

She peeked inside then studied him.

"Why are you doing this?"

"The way I see it, you saved my life," he said. "You could have shot me. You probably have a story why you were here in the first place. Let's just call it a draw."

She put the envelope back on his desk.

"I'll leave but I don't want your money," she said.

Three minutes later she was dressed and stepping out the door. She turned before she got all the way out and said, "I'll return your shirt some day."

Wilde smiled.

"You do that. Do you have a name?"

She nodded.

"Alabama," she said. "Alabama Winger."

"Well you take care, Alabama Winger."

"You too."

Then she was gone.

3

Day One
July 15
Tuesday Morning

A t exactly ten, an alarm clock pulled Degare Danton out of a deep sleep with all the subtleness of a T-Rex attack. He punched it off and called room service to have coffee and croissants delivered in fifteen minutes, which is all he needed to shower, shave and dress.

The food arrived two minutes early.

He said "Thanks," in almost-perfect English and gave the woman a healthy tip.

His hair was pitch-black and European long, not American short. Ordinarily he let it hang free but today he parted it on the side, American style, and got it flat to his head. It was a different look but not necessarily a bad one. He had one of those faces that couldn't be ruined no matter what frame he stuck it in.

Every woman in Denver was his right now.

None of them knew it but that was the reality of it, if he cared to bring that reality home to them.

Unfortunately for them, that's not the reason he was here.

He was here for something much more critical.

He downed the food, took one last look in the mirror, blew himself a kiss and headed for the elevator, dressed in a summer-weight wool blend suit with an expensive hang and a tan hat up top.

The hotel was on Wynkoop, just down from Union Station, the shelter of choice for the rich, affluent and relevant as they passed through this part of the world.

To Danton it was nothing.

In fact, although he'd only been in town for almost no time, he'd already seen enough to tell that all of Denver was nothing. It was actually a curiosity that a cow town like this even occupied a space on the same blue sphere that held the likes of Paris.

Paris was it, end of story, period.

Admittedly, there were a few places that held a candle to Paris.

London.

Rome.

Athens.

But even those candles were weak and shined with hardly any light.

Outside the hotel sat one and only one lonely cab, which proved Danton's point about Denver. He slipped into the back, pulled the door shut and said, "Sixteenth and California, please and thank you."

Someone outside rapped on the glass just as the driver turned on the meter and shifted into first.

"Hold on," Danton said.

Standing on the other side of the rap was an Asian woman.

Even through the glass she was stunning.

Thick black hair.

Moist lips.

Mysterious eyes.

Gorgeous golden skin.

Dressed for success.

She opened the door, looked nervously at her watch and said, "Are you heading downtown by any chance?"

Yes.

He was.

"Can we share the ride, I'll pay."

He scooted over.

"Sure, no problem."

"Thanks, you just saved my life."

He smiled.

"That's good. It looks like a life worth saving."

Danton kept the woman in the corner of his eye but said nothing, getting ready for some clever words when she finally broke down and made a move.

She didn't make a move, however.

Instead she kept her face pointed ahead.

She wore a perfume that could have been French.

Very sensual.

Not too strong.

Her nylons ruffled when she moved her legs.

Downtown the cabbie dropped Danton off, the woman looked in his direction just enough to say, "Thanks again," and that was it. At the last second, Danton asked how far she was going then paid the cabbie to get her there, plus a tip. She said, "Thanks," and disappeared from his life.

Sixteenth Street was bustling with the proportionate vigor of

Champs-Elysees. Danton stepped back against a building out of the way and checked his wrist.

10:28 a.m.

He had two minutes to kill.

He could still smell the woman's perfume and hear the rustling of her nylons.

When he closed his eyes he could taste her lips.

He should have gotten her number.

4

Day One
July 15
Tuesday Morning

Yardley Savannah was a lawyer but not a big-time one, meaning her ratty, one-room law office had no air conditioning, hence the sticky downtown heat would radiate through her windows later today with full intent and opportunity to beat her senseless, once again, for the tenth day straight. She already pictured herself walking over to the window fan, lifting her skirt and letting the wind blow up her 28-year-old legs.

Hot.

Hot.

Hot.

Too hot.

She tossed the morning paper on her desk, got the coffee going and checked her face in the mirror. A mildly but not wildly attractive woman stared back, a woman with black glasses, light brown hair, a good nose and white teeth. She did a little repair to her blush but stopped midstream.

Something was off.

It was almost as if someone had been inside the office.

She looked around for something out of place.

There was nothing evident.

Still, the feeling was inescapable.

Did someone break in?

If so, why?

There was nothing worth taking, except maybe the Royal, but even that had a sticky e key, so it would almost be a blessing if it disappeared.

It hadn't, though.

There it was, sitting right there in the middle of her desk.

She walked over to it, hit the b key three times, then looked around some more.

If someone had broken in, they hadn't left any marks.

She opened the paper and saw something shocking on the front page. Grace Somerfield got murdered Saturday night.

Damn.

Yardley had met her in the lobby once last year, back when she still worked at Denver's largest law firm, Bender, Littlepage & Price, P.C., before she went solo.

Grace was a good person.

Whoever killed her needed to rot in hell.

5

Day One
July 15
Tuesday Morning

Danton's contact didn't show up at 10:30 or even 10:35 for that matter. He punched a phone booth, paced, and decided he'd give the guy five more minutes.

That was all.

Five minutes.

Then—*poof!*—he'd be gone.

Four minutes later the Asian bombshell from the cab walked up and said, "I'm your contact."

"You?"

"Yes."

"I don't get it," Danton said.

"You mean the cab?"

Right.

The cab.

"I was scoping you out," she said. "I'm particular about who I work with."

Danton smiled and shook his head.

"I take it I passed," he said.

"You passed enough to get this far," she said. "Whether you get any further remains to be seen. Tell me what the project's about."

"What's your name?"

She hesitated then said, "Ying."

"Ying?"

"Right, Ying."

"Have you had breakfast yet?"

"I don't eat breakfast," she said. "I'll take some coffee though."

They ended up in a booth at a nice place called the Paramount Café where coffee cups were five times bigger than what Paris served. Ying took a careful sip, studied Danton and leaned forward. "Tell me about the project."

Danton shrugged.

"The project is pretty simple," he said. "It's to find a woman named Emmanuelle Martin."

"Emmanuelle," Ying said. "Is she French?"

Danton nodded.

"Your wife?"

"No."

"Your lover?"

Danton narrowed his eyes.

"Occasionally," Danton said. "That pretty much came to an end a few days ago when she tried to kill me."

"She tried to kill you?"

He nodded.

"Why?"

"It's complicated," he said.

"Were you cheating on her?"

He grinned.

"No, nothing like that," he said. "She was a lover but only when it was convenient for her. We weren't exclusive by any means. Like I said, it's complicated."

Ying wasn't impressed.

"Un-complicate it for me," she said.

"Trust me, none of what you're asking is relevant," Danton said.

Ying almost got up and left.

"What happens when we find her?" Ying asked. "Are you going to kill her? Are you going to teach her a lesson for messing with you?"

"Would that be a problem?"

"Not really."

"You wouldn't care if I killed her?"

"People kill people," she said. "It's none of my business."

"That's pretty cold," he said.

"I don't make the temperature," she said. "I just dress for it."

A waitress swung past with a pitcher and topped off their cups. Danton said, "Thanks," then refocused on Ying. "If she finds out I'm looking for her, that will be her thought, that I'm trying to hunt her down for revenge. Actually, the reason I'm trying to find her is the exact opposite."

"Meaning what?"

"Meaning I'm here to save her."

"From who?"

"From someone who's going to kill her."

"Who?"

"A hitman." He pulled an envelope out of his suit pocket and slid it across the table to her. "That's half," he said. "You get the other half when we find her."

Ying stuffed the envelope in her purse.

"Do you have a picture of her?"

He pulled one out of his wallet.

Ying studied it and said, "She's pretty."

6

Day One
July 15
Tuesday Noon

Shortly before noon, Yardley locked her Blake Street office, maneuvered her five-foot-two frame down the wooden stairway and got dumped into a dirt alley. From there she walked over to 16th Street in the heart of downtown, where she hugged the shady side of the street and threw a penny into the cup of every third beggar. A string of cars rattled up and down the street and spit plumes of smoke at anything that looked like it had lungs.

Up ahead was the tallest building in Denver, the Daniels Fisher Tower, which coincidentally housed the biggest law firm in the city—Bender, Littlepage & Price, P.C.—a firm that had air conditioning, tons of it, so much in fact that half the lawyers had to keep their windows cracked to keep from freezing to death. Yardley knew because she worked in that meat grinder for two years before it fully dawned on her that the paycheck wasn't worth it.

She left last year, almost to the day.

Taylor Lee still worked there.

Taylor Lee was a lot tougher than her.

Just about everyone was, for that matter.

Mike's Eatery was between 16th and 17th, on Welton. Yardley crossed her heart to help ensure the air conditioning would be working, then opened a glass door and stepped inside. A cold blast hit her in the face and made the corners of her lips turn up ever so slightly.

Oh, yeah.

This is what she was talking about.

She looked around, spotted Taylor Lee at a back booth and headed over. The woman looked exactly as she should, namely too good, with her 26-year-old dangerous-dame face, her curvy body and those incredible raven-black locks, styled with high-cut Bettie Page bangs. Right now not much of that body showed, given the fact that she was in lawyer mode.

She pushed an iced-tea across the table as Yardley slid in.

Cold.

Delicious.

Slurpy good.

"One more day," Yardley said, wedging her purse against the wall. "That's the longest I can wait for this heat to break. After that I'm going to go out somewhere and buy a gun, then wipe the sweat off my forehead one last time and start shooting everything in sight."

Taylor smiled.

"Come back to the firm. The door's open. The air conditioner's running." She paused and added, "You can get some new clothes."

Yardley took a sip of tea and tilted her head.

"The meat's grinding, too."

Taylor nodded.

"There is that." A pause, then, "So, how's life on the out-side? Are you making it work?"

Yardley shrugged.

"Some days are better than others. It helps that I've learned how to survive on insects. Believe it or not, everything you need to know about bug nutrition is right there in the Encyclopedia Britannica, under Insects, not Survival. I read this morning that Grace Somerfield got murdered. Was she still using the firm for her legal work?"

Taylor nodded.

"Not me personally, but some of the uppity-ups," she said.

"I met her in the lobby once," Yardley said. "She was friend-ly."

They ordered chicken salads and got their tea topped off.

Halfway through the meal a movement in Yardley's peripheral vision caught her attention. She looked up just as a man set a package on the table. He didn't say a word and left as quickly as he came.

What the hell?

She looked at Taylor.

"Is that for you?"

"Not that I know of."

"Me either," Yardley said.

The package was a brown, cardboard box the size of a breadbox. All the corners were taped shut. There was no writing on it. There was, however, an envelope taped to the top. Taylor pulled it off and opened it to find a typed letter inside:

I will be hiring you as my attorney. What's inside the box pertains to my case. Please keep it safe until we can meet. If you do not hear from me by noon on Wednesday, that means I'm dead.

Yardley picked up the box to gauge the weight, which she estimated to be fifteen or twenty pounds.

"So is this mystery client yours or mine?"

Taylor held her hands up in uncertainty.

"Could be either," she said. "Open the box. Whatever's inside will probably sort it out."

Using a fork, Yardley cut the tape until the top lifted. Something cylindrical was inside, thickly wrapped in cellophane. She found the edge and unwrapped it.

Underneath was something that looked like a rolled up scroll of gold, about 18" wide, length unknown, inscribed with ancient markings.

"Does this relate to you?"

Taylor shook her head.

"No, not even close."

"Me either," Yardley said.

7

Day One
July 15
Tuesday Afternoon

Tuesday afternoon, curiosity made Wilde track down the license plate number of the car parked in front of Neva's on Saturday night, the car that belonged to Grace Somerfield's killer. What he found made his palms sweat. The number, FC211, was registered to a woman named Night Neveraux.

She wasn't a stranger to him.

Anything but.

He stuck a Marlboro in his mouth, lit it, and asked himself a very serious question.

Was Night capable of murder?

The answer surprised him.

Yes, she was.

Damn it.

He bounded down the steps to street level, hopped in the '47 MG/TC, and headed straight to Night's house, which was a rental on Ogden Street between 9th and 10th. Parking on the street was jammed up, but he finally found a spot down near

13th and doubled back on foot.

The sun beat down.

Crazy hot.

He wore the suit jacket for a block then slipped it off and slung it over his shoulder.

Come on, Night.

Be home.

The house was a small red brick structure with no driveway or garage, set in an endless sea of other red brick structures with no driveways or garages.

The windows were open.

A fan was blowing.

Wilde held his breath and knocked on the door.

No one answered.

He knocked again, harder.

Movement came from inside, feet pounding down stairs.

Two heartbeats later the door swung open and Night's 25-year-old face appeared. She wore no makeup, her blond hair was in a ponytail and her face glistened with sweat. She wore a green tank-top and white panties.

"Goddamn you," she said. "What the fuck are you doing here?"

Wilde pulled her stomach to his and licked the sweat off her forehead.

Then he kissed her.

He kissed her like he owned her.

"What do you think?" he said.

He threw her over his shoulder, carried her upstairs and took her like she was the last woman on earth. Afterwards she slapped his face and said, "God I hate you."

He nodded.

"Don't ever stop."

"Don't worry, I won't."

Two minutes later he was back out in the sun walking to the MG.

Fire raced through his veins.

Night had a tattoo behind her ear, the size of a quarter, something new from when he'd last seen her six months ago. Equally bad, a black bag was sitting in the corner of her bedroom. It looked like one of those bags that doctors used. Jewelry was on her nightstand, expensive jewelry, the kind someone like Grace Somerfield would own.

Damn it.

Damn it to hell.

Back at the '47 he fired up the 4-cylinder engine and pointed the roadster's bumperless front end back towards the office. All the bumpy way there he could still taste Night on his tongue and feel her body tremble against his.

He needed to be careful.

Night was a drug.

If he let her back in his blood, it wouldn't be pretty.

8

Day One
July 15
Tuesday Afternoon

D anton's theory was that Emmanuelle Martin would hole up at someplace cheap and out of the way, so Ying drove him around her 1940 Packard Coupe and asked questions at all the right places, leaving a five dollar bill with everyone they talked to.

So far, no one had seen her.

Nor had anyone seen anyone who looked like a hitman or spoke French.

Early afternoon, they stopped by Ying's place to rest and regroup. It was a standalone house a kilometer east of downtown, but that was about the best that could be said about it. It was small, dark and cramped.

"It's a rental," Ying said, lighting a cigarette. "I'm in a savings mode, getting ready to buy in the next year or two."

Danton nodded.

He didn't care.

This was the first time they were alone. His thoughts were on whether they'd end up tearing each other's clothes off. Suddenly something grabbed his attention. It was a photograph in a standup frame on the lamp table. He picked it up and studied it. It was Ying and another equally attractive female with their arms around each other. The background was simple—a window, curtains, a crooked painting, the edge of a lampshade.

"That's me and a friend," Ying said.

"She's pretty."

"Her name was Jessica Dent," Ying said. "She got murdered last year, on May 12th, to be exact."

"You're kidding, right?"

No.

She wasn't.

"Did they ever catch the guy?"

She shook her head.

"That's too bad."

Right.

Too bad.

Ying put a distant look on her face and said, "They found her naked. There were words carved into her chest with a knife."

"Fuck," Danton said. "That's gross."

"They said, *Next time follow directions.*"

"Next time follow directions?"

"Right."

"What's that supposed to mean?"

Ying shrugged.

"No one ever figured it out."

"Weird."

Danton patted the woman's shoulder. "I'll tell you what," he said. "After we get this Emmanuelle business done, I'll look into your friend's case if you want."

"Why, what could you do?"

He shrugged.

"I'm pretty good at figuring things out," he said.

"The cops couldn't figure it out."

"That doesn't mean anything."

Ying got a glass of water from the kitchen then unbuttoned her blouse as she walked towards him. Her mouth was open, her breathing was short and quick, and her eyes belonged to a predator.

Danton grabbed her and pulled her in.

He let her feel his strength.

Then he locked his arms under her legs, picked her up and pinned her against the wall.

She wrapped her legs around him.

Then she kissed him, hard, more like a bite than a kiss.

Danton tasted blood in his mouth and didn't care.

He reached between her legs and ripped her panties off.

Suddenly a door slammed, someone had entered the house, followed by a voice— *"What the fuck!"*

The voice was deep.

A man's.

With Ying still clinging to him, Danton turned.

A man with a cocked arm was charging.

He was big.

Strong.

The fury in his eyes was unmistakable.

Before Danton could react, the fist smashed into his face and he dropped to the floor.

Pain exploded.

Colors flashed.

He struggled to get up.

It did no good.

His brain didn't focus.

His body didn't respond.

Then a violent kick landed on the side of his head.

9

Day One
July 15
Tuesday Afternoon

S ince the mystery client intended to hire either Yardley or Taylor, but they had no idea which, they flipped a coin to determine who should take custody of the scroll on an interim basis. Yardley lost, meaning she had to take it.

She carried it under her arm back to her office, locked the door and unrolled it.

It turned out to be ten feet long, inscribed with markings from end to end. The markings were all straight lines and looked as if they'd been made using a hammer and chisel. Yardley placed a sheet of paper at the top end and colored it in lightly with pencil to record the markings, which came out lighter than their surroundings. She repeated that all the way down, until she had a complete image of the scroll on eleven sheets of paper. She rolled the scroll up, put the cellophane around it and stuck it back in the box.

There.

Good as new.

Now, where to keep it?

She didn't have a safe in her office or her apartment. At this point no one knew she had it except Taylor, but if it was real gold—which it seemed to be—she needed to be careful. It was worth a fortune even if it turned out to be something modern, without historical significance.

She didn't want to leave it in the office after having the feeling this morning that someone had broken in, so she took it to her fourth-floor apartment down the street, removed the scroll from the box, wrapped it in tin foil and stuck it in the freezer behind as much stuff as she could.

The empty box went under her bed.

Good enough.

She latched all her windows from the inside, made sure her door was locked good and tight, then headed for the trolley with the eleven sheets of paper folded up inside her purse.

She was on a mission.

A mission to find out what the markings said.

10

Day One
July 15
Tuesday Afternoon

When Wilde got back to the office from Night's house, Alabama Winger was sitting on the sidewalk outside the building next to a beggar, waiting for him.

"Surprise," she said.

"That's an understatement," Wilde said. "Come on up."

Inside he turned on the radio and twisted the dial. About the best he could find was an old Paul Williams song, "The Hucklebuck," and left it there.

He lit a cigarette and offered one to Alabama.

"No thanks," she said.

"What, you don't smoke?"

"I do but only when I'm on fire."

Wilde grinned.

Before he could ask the woman what was on her mind, the phone rang and the velvety voice of Leigh Monroe came through. Wilde pulled up an image of her doll face and sultry ways. "Well look who actually answers the phone every now and then," she said.

"You been calling?"

"Hell yes I've been calling," she said. "John's sister died this morning back in Chicago. He's heading there as we speak. That puts yours truly up the unsanitary tributary without any means of propulsion for a gig tonight."

Wilde didn't need her to decode it.

Leigh was Denver's best blues singer, one of the few in the world who actually rivaled Billie Holliday, at least in Wilde's opinion. John was the group's drummer. Wilde was Denver's go-to drummer whenever a group needed a fill-in. He was also the most sought-after studio drummer in town.

"Where you playing tonight?" he asked.

"The Bokaray."

The Bokaray

That was a nice place, full of smoke, sinners and sex.

"Okay, I'll see you there," Wilde said. "Regular time?"

"Right, regular time," Leigh said. "The drinks are on me. I owe you one."

"One? What kind of math are you using?"

Leigh laughed.

"Bye bye, lover."

The line went dead.

Wilde turned to Alabama and said, "So what's on your mind, Alabama Winger?"

She diverted her eyes.

"I want you to hire me," she said. "I want to be your Girl Friday."

Wilde chewed on it.

He didn't need the help.

He couldn't afford to feed a mouth.

Well, that wasn't exactly true.

He could but it would stretch him.

"Why?"

"I don't want to be on the streets any more. I want to be normal. You're the only nice person I've met in a month."

Wilde walked to the window and looked down.

Larimer Street buzzed.

It was stronger than Alabama.

It would kill her in time.

"I already did my first job for you," Alabama said.

Wilde turned.

"What does that mean?"

"Well, when you were meeting with that woman this morning, I was in the other room," she said.

"I know that."

"I heard everything that you both said," Alabama said. "I know you didn't want to be the substitute witness like she wanted. So I did it for you."

"What do you mean?"

"I called the police and pretended I was up on Capitol Hill on Saturday night," she said. "I told them I saw a blond woman running out of a yard. I told them about the tattoo behind the woman's ear and about the license plate number, FC211. I told them the story just like that woman wanted you to tell it."

Wilde mashed the butt in the ashtray.

"Did you give them your name?"

"I gave them a name, but not my name," she said. "I told them my name was Sandra Winger."

"You used your correct last name?"

"Right, but the wrong first name." She paused for a moment and added, "Well, to be technically correct, that actually is my real first name. Alabama's my nickname. So, do I get the job?"

Suddenly the import of what she did solidified in Wilde's brain.

This was bad.

Worse than bad.

He grabbed her hand, dragged her towards the door and said, "Come on."

She fell into step.

"Where we going?"

Wilde didn't answer.

He bounded down the stairs two at a time with the woman in tow. At street level he turned and said, "I'm half tempted to hire you just so I can fire you."

In the MG she said, "You're not a very nice boss so far."

He cranked up the engine, jammed the shifter into first and said, "Yeah, well, get used to it."

"Does that mean I'm hired?"

"Yeah, you're hired," he said, pulling into traffic.

"Thank you."

"Now you're fired."

She looked confused.

"Sorry, I just had to do that," he said. "Now you're rehired."

"So am I working for you or not?"

"It looks that way."

She laid her head on his shoulder and squeezed his arm. Then she straightened up and said, "I can't type, just so we're clear on that."

"Girl Friday's are supposed to type."

"Well yours doesn't."

11

Day One
July 15
Tuesday Afternoon

It took Danton seven minutes to kill the man, seven full minutes that were without a doubt the longest, most painful and frantic minutes of his life. He collapsed when it was over and didn't move, too brutally exhausted to even try to figure out how badly he was broken. Ying wrapped her arms over him for a few minutes, then got a wet towel and wiped blood off his face. Danton got enough strength to sit up and lean against the wall.

He looked at the body.

"Your boyfriend, I assume."

"No."

"No?"

"He's an asshole who managed to get his hooks in me," she said. "I'm glad he's dead. We'll wait until after dark and dump his body. I know a place."

Danton grunted.

"Remind me to not get on your bad side," he said.

She kissed him.

Slowly.

Softly.

"Likewise," she said.

Her phone rang. She got quiet while someone on the other end did the talking, then she said, "Thanks, you done good," and hung up.

"That was one of our five-dollar guys from this morning, the one at the Bright Star. A Frenchwoman just checked in under the name Nicole Wickliff," she said. "Does she ring a bell?"

"Not by name," Danton said. "I'll need to get a look at her but I can already tell you the chance of her not being the person who's going to kill Emmanuelle is zero."

"Two French people in Denver at the same time," Ying said. "I'll bet that's never happened before."

Danton agreed.

"She wouldn't be checking in if she'd already killed her," he said. "At least we have that going for us." He refocused on the body. "What's his name?"

"Michael Spencer."

"Michael Spencer," he said to the body. "Nice to meet you."

12

Day One
July 15
Tuesday Afternoon

Edward Berkley was about sixty with bifocals, Einstein hair and no wedding ring. His office, a clutter of twenty years in the making, was in the bowels of the museum. His smile was skinny and his voice was weak. His eyes never met Yardley's for more than a heartbeat before darting away.

"So let's see what you have," he said.

Yardley pulled the eleven sheets of paper out of her purse and passed them across the desk.

"This is it," she said.

"Okay."

"I'm pretty sure it's Egyptian."

"Well, let's have a look."

"Thanks again. I really appreciate this."

"No problem."

Berkley studied every page, then pulled a magnifying glass out of a drawer and focused with even greater intent. Occasionally he peeked over the top of his glasses at Yardley but didn't say anything.

She waited.

Silently.

Finally Berkley looked up and said, "This isn't Egyptian."

"It's not?"

"No, none of it."

"What is it?"

"It's Greek," he said.

"Can you interpret it?"

He shook his head.

"No, it's old—maybe even dating B.C.—but it's still Greek. That's a language I don't know much about, other than to recognize it when I see it. Sorry."

13

Day One
July 15
Tuesday Afternoon

Wilde screeched to a halt was in front of Night's house and turned to Alabama. "Can you drive a car?"

"Yes."

He left the engine running and hopped out.

"See that house right there?" he said, pointing. "There's an alley that runs behind it. Take the car back around there and wait for me."

"You got it."

Wilde ran to the front door.

Grinding gears made him turn and look back to find Alabama trying to get the vehicle into first. The engine conked out, the woman fired it up again and got the car moving with a sudden jerk.

Wilde winced and knocked on the door.

No one answered.

He turned the knob and entered.

"Night!"

She appeared at the top of the stairs, visibly startled, as Wilde ran up two at a time, grabbed her shoulders and shook her.

"Listen to me and listen fast," he said. "There's a rumor on the street that you might be involved in the murder of Grace Somerfield."

Her face wrinkled.

"Who in the hell ..."

"No questions," he said. "Just listen. There's a possibility that the cops are going to be showing up here to search the place. If you have anything in the house that ties you to the crime, get it out of here right now this second."

Her eyes darted.

She ran into the bedroom, grabbed the jewels on the nightstand and threw them into the bag in the corner, the one that looked like a doctor's bag. Then she reached under the bed, pulled out a shoebox and dumped the contents into the bag.

Sirens came up the street.

Night jammed the bag into Wilde's hands and said, "Take it."

He hesitated.

"Please!"

He gripped it hard, ran out the back door, jumped into the passenger seat of the MG and told Alabama, "Go."

She ground into first and squealed the wheels.

14

Day One
July 15
Tuesday Afternoon

D anton stuffed Spencer's lifeless form in the basement until tonight, then hopped in the shower to
wash the fight off. He had more bruises on his arms
and torso than the law allowed, plus a massive swelling under
his hair, but he'd kept his face fairly well protected. A couple
of minor cuts showed, that was it.

They headed over to the Bright Starr where the French
woman had checked in and parked a block down the street
near Wynkoop.

Ying left the keys in the ignition and said, "Wait here."

"I should be doing this, not you."

"Just relax and let me earn my keep," Ying said, getting out.
Before she shut the door she added, "After we dump Spencer's
body tonight, we should go to this club I know and get drunk."

"What kind of club?"

"It's called the Bokaray," she said. "Leigh Monroe's singing
there tonight."

"Is she good?"

"She's sexy."

She closed the door, blew him a kiss and disappeared down the street.

Drunken sex.

That's what he'd have tonight.

Drunken sex.

There was nothing better.

They needed to be careful dumping Spencer's body, though. The last thing they needed was let Spencer bite them in the ass. The little finger on Danton's left hand was stiff and swollen, either sprained or broken.

No big deal.

Ying was gone for a full half hour but came back excited. "Our friend was out of the room and the five-dollar guy let me in, for ten more dollars," she said. "The big thing I found was a picture of Emmanuelle in her suitcase. There's no question that Emmanuelle's the reason the woman's in town."

"Good job."

"There's more," she said. "The five-dollar guy said he had some more news for me, but it would cost another ten dollars."

"Did you pay it?"

She nodded.

"It was worth it," she said. "The story is, this Nicole woman asked where she could buy a gun in town, on the side. The five-dollar guy told her to contact a man named Lloyd."

"Who's Lloyd?"

"I don't know," Ying said. "I never heard of him. All I know is what the five-dollar guy told our friend Nicole that Lloyd stays in a flophouse on Larimer Street. His room is on the fourth floor, above a bar called Mile-High Whiskey."

Danton chewed on it.

"Wait here," he said, stepping out.

"Where you going?"

"Our five-dollar guy's turning into a greedy man," he said. "He's already leveraged this thing up to twenty-five. His next move is to approach Nicole and let her know he has some great information to tell her—meaning me and you—for ten or twenty or thirty dollars. I'm going to go have a talk with him and let him know the consequences of getting too greedy."

Ying grabbed his arm.

"Let me do it," she said.

"Why?"

"I'm going to convey the message but I'm also going to pay him the other thirty right now," she said.

"It won't do any good," Danton said.

"We'll see," she said. "If it doesn't, then I don't care if you kill him. He had his chance."

15

Day One
July 15
Tuesday Afternoon

Although Edward Berkley couldn't interpret the scroll, he called Blanche Twister, Ph.D., over at the University of Denver to see if she might be up to the task.

"I'd be happy to look at it," Twister said. "No guarantees though."

Yardley headed over.

The campus was buzzing, still packed with war vets taking advantage of the G.I Bill.

Twister turned out to be a conservatively dressed woman in her early fifties. She had an easy smile, kind eyes and a clean office except for the walls, which were covered with ancient maps. Yardley handed her the eleven pages then leaned back in the chair and watched.

Twister flipped through the pages rapidly, looked up and said, "This is written in the form of Greek that was spoken by the Hellenic aristocracy from about 300 B.C. forward. Basically, it's five separate descriptions of locations where something is buried. It's strange though in that none of the starting points are described or identified. Here's the interesting thing," she said, pointing to the bottom of the last page. "Do you know what that says?"

No.

She didn't.

"It says, Cleopatra," Twister said.

"It's about Cleopatra?"

"No, not about her," Twister said. "That's her signature. This was written by her, if it's genuine."

"Do you think it is, genuine?"

"I'd have to see the original," Twister said. "But everything here fits. Cleopatra—formally Cleopatra VII Philopator—was the last Egyptian pharaoh of the Ptolemaic dynasty. Although she bore the ancient Egyptian title of pharaoh, the Ptolemic dynasty was Hellenistic. As such, Cleopatra's language was the Greek spoken by the Hellenic aristocracy, not Egyptian. That's what this is written in. If Cleopatra wrote something, this is exactly what it would look like."

"Interesting," Yardley said.

Twister smiled. "This is so far past interesting that it's not even funny," she said.

"So what do you think it means?"

Twister spun around in her chair, full circle, three times.

Then she said, "I can speculate if you want me to."

Yardley nodded.

"Please do."

16

Day One
July 15
Tuesday Afternoon

Wilde chain-smoked as he paced back and forth in front of the windows, occasionally throwing a glance at the black bag sitting in the middle of his desk, Night's black bag to be precise, Night's black bag filled with Grace Somerfield's stolen jewels and valuables to be even more precise.

Damn it.

One split-second decision.

That's all it took to ruin his life.

"I'm technically an accessory after the fact," he told Alabama. "I don't think you're anything at this point. All you did was drive and you didn't really know anything that was going on." He blew a smoke ring and said, "If I were you, I'd just walk out that door right now and never look back."

She cocked her head.

"That's a lie."

"What's a lie?"

"When you said if you were me you'd walk out the door,"

she said. "If you were me, you wouldn't walk out the door. That's the last thing you'd do."

"What makes you say that?"

"Because that's not what you did when Night needed you," she said. "You stuck by her even though you had to get dirty to do it."

"That was just a stupid, bad decision on my part," Wilde said. "If I would have had ten seconds to reflect on what I was doing I wouldn't have done it."

"That's another lie," Alabama said.

Wilde almost debated it but realized she'd never let him win.

"So what are you going to do with all the stuff?" Alabama asked. "Just give it back to Night?"

Wilde shrugged.

Good question.

"I don't know."

He walked over and locked the door, just so no one would bust in and see the bag sitting on the desk. Good thing, too, because three minutes later the knob turned and someone tried to enter.

Wilde handed the bag to Alabama and said, "Take this in the next room and hide it."

Someone pounded at the door.

"Wilde, are you in there?"

He recognized the voice.

It belonged to Detective Warner Raven, the head of the homicide department.

Shit!

He whispered to Alabama, "Don't make a sound," then closed the door between the two rooms and let the detective in.

Warner Raven's gun showed through his suit jacket. It was still in the holster, though, and he didn't have a group of cops behind him. He had a hard, manly face with a cleft chin and a morning shadow. As far as hunters went, he was the best Denver had seen in the last twenty years. He took off his hat, tossed it at the rack and got a ringer.

"It's called finesse," he said.

Wilde lit another cigarette and held the pack towards Raven, who declined.

"It's called luck," Wilde said.

"Maybe a little."

"So what's the occasion?"

"The occasion is murder," Raven said. "Ugly, ugly murder."

17

Day One
July 15
Tuesday Afternoon

L loyd the gun dealer wasn't home so Danton and Ying caught a late lunch at a dirty spoon across the street while they kept an eye on the building.

"Tell me about Spencer," Danton said. "You said he had his hooks in you. How?"

Ying frowned, deciding, then looked into Danton's eyes.

"It's a pretty simple story," she said. "I did something I wasn't supposed to, something illegal, not a little illegal, a lot illegal. Nothing happened for two years and I actually almost forgot about it. Then one day out of the blue, two men showed up at my door. One was Spencer and the other was his buddy, Kent Dawson. They saw what I did and spent the next two years tracking me down. They wanted to arrange a deal."

"What kind of deal?"

"Their silence in exchange for favors," Ying said. "They ran in high circles and needed an escort or two for important people when they came to town. They didn't want the ordinary city whore, though. They wanted someone classy and pure."

"You."

She nodded.

"I'm going to tell you something I shouldn't," she said. "If you hate me after I tell you, I'm not going to blame you."

Danton ran his fingers through his hair.

"That's not going to happen."

"You haven't heard what I'm about to tell you yet," Ying said.

"Then do tell so I can prove myself right."

She chewed salad, swallowed and said, "This morning, I was supposed to show up for an escort deal, which got set up late last night, after Sam Poppenberg called me with the assignment to help you. I decided to scope you out, which explains the cab ride this morning, to see how tough you were. I knew either Spencer or Dawson would come looking for me after I stood them up. I also knew that if you were with me at the time, there'd be a confrontation."

Danton shifted his body.

"So you set me up."

She nodded.

Her eyes got wet and she put her hand on his.

"I'm sorry," she said. "I really am. The problem is that they've been in my life for so long. I had to get them out and I had to do it in a way that they didn't know I was doing it, in case it didn't work."

Danton tilted his head.

"You got some nerve to tell me, I'll give you that."

"To be honest, if Spencer was the only problem, I wouldn't be telling you anything," she said. "The reason I'm telling you is that Dawson's still out there. By the end of the day, he'll figure out that something happened to Spencer. He'll coming looking to see if I had anything to do with it. He's ten times worse than Spencer. He's got the eyes of a rattlesnake. I don't want you to get blindsided by him. I need to tell you the truth so you have the chance to get away from me, if that's what you choose to do."

"That's not what I choose to do," Danton said. "So relax."

18

Day One
July 15
Tuesday Afternoon

Blanche Twister, Ph.D., got up and shut the door. Then she collected her thoughts and told Yardley, "In 31 B.C., Cleopatra was the reigning pharaoh of Egypt. At that time she had Mark Antony at her side and was preparing for an impending attack on Alexandria by the Romans under the command of Octavian. Antony's forces eventually faced the Romans in a naval action off the coast of Actium, which later became known as the Battle of Actium. Antony's fleet, which was poorly equipped and manned, lost resoundingly. Alexandria fell and both Antony and Cleopatra ended up committing suicide shortly thereafter. The rumor is that Cleopatra enraged a viper until it bit her. In any event, her two children, then ages six and ten, were spared and taken to Rome where they lived out their lives."

"Okay."

"A lot of Cleopatra's treasures and valuables were recovered by Octavian," Twister said. "There has always been a historical question, though, as to whether all of her riches were there."

She scratched her ear.

"So far, everything I've told you is fairly well documented," she said. "Now, you asked me to speculate, so here's where the speculation part starts. Put yourself in Cleopatra's shoes. There you are, about to embark on a war you'll probably lose. You have two children, ages six and ten. You don't want your valuables to fall into enemy hands. Does this make sense?"

"It does."

"So what do you do?" Twister asked. "If I was Cleopatra, I'd take a small group of trusted men and bury my most precious valuables where nobody would find them. If by chance I won the war, I'd go back and get them, and just hope that the men I thought were trustworthy actually were. If I lost, however, at least my hated enemy wouldn't get my treasures and maybe, just maybe, there would be a way to get them into the hands of my children down the road."

"And that's the scroll," Yardley said.

"Precisely," Twister said. "I think what we have here is the metes and bounds descriptions of five different sites where Cleopatra buried her riches just before the Battle of Actium. The reason the five different starting points aren't described on the scroll is because Cleopatra had them in her head. If she wrote them down, anyone who came across the scroll would be able to find them."

"So what do you think she did with the scroll?"

"I think she buried it in a safe place that only she and Antony and her two children knew about," Twister said. "I think it's been buried for the last two thousand years and that the world never knew it existed."

"It's got to be worth a fortune," Yardley said.

Twister frowned.

"Make no mistake about that," she said. "There are five hundred people in Denver right now, not even counting the rest of the world, who would slit your throat in a heartbeat to lay their hands on that scroll if they knew it existed. My advice to you is to not utter a single word about it to anyone."

"Edward Berkley knows about it," Yardley said.

"He doesn't know what it is," Twister said. "All he knows is that you have some sheets of paper that are in ancient Greek and you came to see me about them. You didn't tell him about the scroll itself, if I understand you."

"That's correct."

"Okay, good. After you leave, I'm going to call him and tell him that the papers you brought me to look at were nothing of importance, but thanks for the referral anyway."

Yardley pictured the scroll in her freezer.

Unattended.

"How much do you think it's worth?"

Twister wrinkled her forehead.

"Obviously just the gold alone is worth a small fortune," she said. "What makes it priceless, though, is the historical significance. If it really is what it purports to be, this is undoubtedly one of the most significant archeological finds in the last two thousand years. More importantly, it might even lead to the discovery of the five burial sites. Now that would be almost unthinkable."

"How could the scroll lead to the sites?" Yardley said. "Without the starting points, the metes and bounds descriptions are useless. The critical part of the secret died when Cleopatra died."

Twister stood up and paced.

Then she looked at Yardley and said, "Maybe yes and maybe

no. The more I think about it, the more I wonder if the starting points might have existed someplace in writing, in a second scroll perhaps, a scroll that only listed the starting points but not the metes and bounds descriptions."

"So what you're saying is that maybe all the information is there, but it's split into two separate scrolls."

Twister nodded.

"It's a possibility. Remember, this is all just wild speculation."

"I wonder where the second scroll would be."

A pigeon landed on the windowsill.

Twister shoed it away.

"If we knew where the first scroll was discovered, that might provide a clue as to where the second one is, if indeed there is such a thing," Twister said. "Do you know where the one you have was found?"

No.

She didn't.

"Find out," Twister said. "I assume it was in Alexandria somewhere, but it may have been somewhere along the Mediterranean coast or even up the Nile."

19

Day One
July 15
Tuesday Afternoon

As the detective got comfortable in a chair, Wilde stole a glance out the window to see if cop cars were below. None were. "I'm going to show you something that no one outside the homicide department has ever seen," Raven said.

"Okay."

Raven reached into his suit pocket, pulled out a half-dozen photographs and slid them across the desk.

They depicted a woman.

A naked woman.

A naked woman with her hands tied behind her back.

Dead.

Brutally dead with a bloody slit throat.

That wasn't the strange part though.

Words had been carved in her stomach.

Wilde tried to read them but couldn't.

"They say, *Next time follow instructions*," Raven said. "The victim's name is Jessica Dent. She was killed eighteen months ago.

We never figured out who did it."

Wilde put the photos on the desk face down.

"Why are you showing me these?"

Raven pulled a pack of Marlboros out of his shirt pocket, tapped two out, handed one to Wilde and lit them up with a silver lighter.

"In May of last year, I got a telephone call out of the blue," Raven said. "It was a man's voice, one I didn't recognize. He was talking through a handkerchief or something like that, disguising it. He said, *You will die on Friday*. Then he hung up."

"You will die on Friday?"

"Right, *You will die on Friday*," Raven said. "Those were the exact words. The call came on a Tuesday."

Wilde blew smoke.

"So what'd you do?"

"My first instinct was that someone was just fucking with me," Raven said. "When word got around the department, though, people started to get pissed that a threat like that would be levied against one of their kind. They took the matter seriously and resolved to catch the guy."

Wilde nodded.

"Sounds reasonable," he said. "It might have been a joke but you never know."

"Anyway, we pulled all the cases I'd been working on for the last five years and went through them, looking for someone who was pissed enough to kill me, maybe a relative of someone I arrested, or someone in the family of a murder victim where the killer never got caught, that kind of thing."

"What'd you find?"

"We found a few things worth further investigation," Raven said. "We didn't have much time to run them down, however.

As Friday approached, our plan changed. We decided to just wait and see if someone actually made an attempt to kill me and catch him in the act."

"Okay."

The radio was playing lightly in the background.

It was a hillbilly song.

Wilde flicked it off.

"Judging by the fact that you're sitting in my chair, I'm going to guess that the guy wasn't successful."

"You'd be wrong," Raven said.

"Huh?"

"On Wednesday of that week, a woman went missing," Raven said. "Her name was Jessica Dent. The homicide department didn't even know about it. Why would we? It wasn't a case in our purview. Anyway, Friday rolled around and the guy called me at home after dark. He told me to go to the phone booth at 15th and Curtis and wait for a call. He also said, *Here's the important part. Come alone. Don't try any tricks. Don't try to catch me.*"

"Yeah, right," Wilde said. "Fat chance of that."

"Exactly," Raven said. "We got four cops in plain clothes to flank the area. The thinking was that the guy was going to call me and give me directions to go somewhere. The guys would follow me wherever I went, laying low and keeping a distance, of course."

"Good plan," Wilde said.

Raven took one last drag on the Marlboro and mashed the butt in the ashtray.

"Actually it wasn't," he said. "The phone never rang. Jessica Dent's body showed up next to the BNSF tracks on the north edge of the city Saturday morning. What was carved in her stomach—*Next time follow directions*—was obviously directed at me."

"Damn."

"Right, damn," Raven said. "We ran down the leads we pulled up earlier in the week but none of them panned out. Jessica Dent turned into a cold case. I've thought about her every day since it happened."

Raven walked to the windows, looked down and said, "I love Larimer Street."

Wilde grinned.

"That's because half your work comes from here."

Raven shrugged.

"You may be right," he said. "Here's the reason I'm here. An hour ago, I got a call from my friend. It was the exact same voice as before with the exact same words, *You will die on Friday.*"

"So he's playing his game again."

"Right," Raven said. "I haven't told anyone in the department and I don't intend to. The only person I'm telling is you. What I want you to do is find out who he is."

Raven pulled an envelope out of his suit pocket and set it on the desk.

"That's a thousand dollars."

Wilde looked at it.

A thousand dollars.

That was three months salary.

"From your own pocket?"

Raven nodded.

"I want this guy."

Wilde tilted his head. "Keep your money," he said. "This one's on the house."

Raven lit another cigarette. "Thanks, but I want you motivated. The important thing is for you to stay off this guy's radar screen. You need to find him without him knowing you're doing it."

Wilde chewed on it.

"Has he taken anyone yet?"

"No one that I'm aware of," Raven said. "Jessica Dent was taken on a Wednesday, so maybe tomorrow's the day. Anyone who goes missing, I'll make you aware of it right away."

Wilde nodded.

"You do that," he said. "I'll need access to all your old files."

"I was afraid you were going to say that."

"Is it possible?"

"No, you're a civilian," Raven said. "I'll have to sneak them out of the office. Give me a couple of hours to figure out how."

He stood up and headed for the door, leaving the photos and the money on the desk. Before he got out Wilde said, "Hey, Raven."

The man stopped and turned.

"What are you going to do if I don't find him?"

"If that happens, it will just be me and him on Friday," Raven said.

Wilde frowned.

"He'll kill you."

"Maybe."

"He'll still kill the woman," Wilde said. "You realize that, I hope. Maybe he's saying it to you, *You will die on Friday,* but he's saying it to her too."

"You don't know that."

"That's why he takes her early in the week," Wilde said, "so he can sit back and watch her contemplate her death for a few days."

20

Day One
July 15
Tuesday Afternoon

The more Danton envisioned an impending attack by Kent Dawson, the more he didn't want it to happen while there was a dead body in the basement.

An alley ran behind the house.

Ying got the Packard as close to the back door as she could, opened the truck and surveyed the area for nosy neighbors. She saw none, either in the area or looking out windows, and rapped on the back door.

"Come on."

Danton stepped out with the body under one arm, wrapped in a blanket. He dumped it in the trunk as fast as he could and slammed the lid.

Then they got the hell out of there.

"I don't think anyone saw us," Ying said.

"Time will tell."

Thirty minutes later they were on an abandoned gravel service road that ran next to railroad tracks. Two miles down, Ying brought the Packard to a stop.

"Here?" Danton said.

It was a little too out in the open for his comfort zone.

"Remember when I told you about my friend Jessica Dent getting murdered?"

Yes.

He remembered.

"This is where the killer dumped her body," Ying said. "Right where we are. I've been back here fifty times. It's always been totally deserted just like it is now." She shifted into first and drove another hundred yards down the road. "We'll dump Spencer here. If by chance anyone sees my car leaving, I'll have an excuse that I was visiting Jessica's site."

"Clever."

They looked around, saw no one and stuffed the body into the cover of a six-foot rabbit brush, taking the blanket with them.

On the way out they encountered no one.

No trains.

No cars.

No walkers.

No nothing.

Five miles down the main road, heading back into the city, Danton threw the blanket out the window and watched it disappear over the side of a bridge.

There.

Done.

When they got back to Ying's, the place was trashed.

Drawers were pulled out and dumped on the floor.

Same for the cupboards.

The couch and chair cushions had been slit open and the

guts pulled out.

Same for the mattress, slit open.

The TV was smashed face down on the carpet.

The back had been pried off.

"This isn't Kent Dawson being pissed off or sending you a message," Danton said. "Someone was looking for something." He locked eyes with Ying and said, "Tell me who it was and what they were looking for."

She wrinkled her forehead.

"If it wasn't Dawson, I don't know who it was."

21

Day One
July 15
Tuesday Afternoon

Yardley sat at a table at the Down Towner Café on 17th Street late Tuesday afternoon and second-guessed the sanity of what she was about to do. The scroll had transformed her. It had been doing it all day and she'd done nothing to stop it. Taylor Lee maneuvered her voluptuous body through the front door at exactly 4:30 p.m. and headed over.

They ordered coffee.

Yardley relayed her meetings today and what she'd learned about the scroll.

Taylor's forehead got tighter and tighter.

When Yardley stopped talking, Taylor said, "The scroll isn't yours and it isn't mine. It belongs to a client. We don't have the right to be making paper imprints of it or having it examined by third parties."

"So, you're mad at me?"

"Not mad," Taylor said. "I'm just saying, you've gone way out of your bounds. I'm a little astonished, to tell you the truth.

I've never seen this side of you before."

"Yeah, well, get used to it," Yardley said.

Taylor leaned back and studied her.

"What does that mean?"

"It means I have a proposition for you."

"This isn't going to a good place, I can already tell," Taylor said.

"Maybe yes, maybe no," Yardley said. "What's been bothering me all day is the way the scroll got dumped on our table so anonymously. Now, why would a client do that?"

Taylor shrugged.

She didn't know.

"I'll tell you why," Yardley said. "Because he stole it. He's using us to safeguard it."

"Could be," Taylor said.

"Here's what I suggest we do," Yardley said. "I suggest that you and me make a pact to join forces. We don't know who the mystery client is yet and whether he belongs to you or me. But we join forces nevertheless, irrespective of whether he eventually belongs to you or to me. Then, when he shows up, we try to confirm that he actually stole it."

"Why?"

"Because then we steal it from him," Yardley said. "Only if he stole it, though. If it turns out he got it legitimately, we return it to him."

Taylor laughed.

"You're kidding, right?"

Yardley finished chewing, took a sip of water and said, "If it turns out he stole it, what's he going to do? He can't file a police report."

"He could kill us," Taylor said. "How about that?"

"He won't know it's us," Yardley said. "What we do is make it disappear innocently in a way that doesn't implicate us. Maybe we set up a charade where it appears to have been stolen from us, something along those lines."

"These are dangerous ideas you're playing with," Taylor said.

"Yeah, I know," Yardley said. "Play it out, though. Suppose he stole it and we do nothing. The scroll will end up hidden from the world. If we take it, though, here's what we do. We keep it secret while we find the second scroll, the one with the starting points. Then we find the five buried treasures. We then keep the treasures and the second scroll, but turn the first scroll over to the proper authorities, where it can be shared with the world. We can turn it over anonymously, without even demanding any money. That way the client will never know it was us who had it."

"You're crazy," Taylor said.

Yardley nodded.

"We need to know where the first scroll was found," she said. "We can't make the scroll disappear and lose the client until we have that information under our belts. Otherwise, we'll never find the second scroll."

Taylor tilted her head.

"What do we do with the second scroll and the five treasures, if we find them?"

"We'll cross that bridge when that bridge comes up in front of us for crossing. One thing we could do is sell them to the proper authorities," Yardley said. "We get rich and everything goes on display for the world to see. Everyone wins. Isn't that worth a little personal risk?"

22

Day One
July 15
Tuesday Afternoon

After the detective left, Alabama came out of the back room and said, "That was a close one. I thought for sure he came here about Grace Somerfield. If he started to take you in, I was getting ready to come innocently into the room, snatch your gun out of the drawer before he knew what was happening and shoot him in the leg."

Wilde pulled $75 out of the envelope.

"First of all, don't ever shoot anyone, especially on my watch, and more especially with my gun. Second of all, what I want you to do is go out and buy some clothes," he said. "Get some day wear, some stalking wear—by which I mean all things black—and get a nice sexy evening dress, plus some nylons that have a line up the back. Get some black high heels, too. Black or red, I don't care."

She took the money.

"Why? What's going on?"

"Lots of stuff," he said. "Go to one of the department

stores on 16th Street."

"You're the boss." She headed for the door. "Hey, Wilde, where do you want me to sleep tonight? With you?"

"What does that mean?"

"It means I've been staying over at the Metropolitan," she said.

Wilde winced.

The Metropolitan Hotel, a block over on Market, was the king of the fleabags, a full flea's head and shoulders above the other bags of flea. It rented closet-sized cubicles for $1 a week, payment in advance, no questions asked. It was one step above the alley but not a giant one.

"We'll figure something out," he said.

She ran a finger down his chest.

"What did you have in mind, exactly, cowboy?"

He lit a cigarette and said, "You're not here to be screwed so get it out of your head. It's not going to happen."

She headed for the door and said over her shoulder, "Yes it is."

Then she was gone.

Suddenly her head stuck back in through the door.

"Caught you picturing it," she said.

Then she was gone again.

She'd be gone a couple of hours. Wilde used the time to hop in the MG and head over to the BNSF line and drive down the service road to where Jessica Dent's body had been dumped in May of last year.

The killer had been there.

It was as good a place as any to start.

Wilde killed the engine and stepped out.

The sun beat down.

The terrain was largely prairie grassland, punctuated with rabbit brush and yucca.

There were hardly any trees.

No one was around.

How did the killer know about this place?

Did he ride his bike back here when he was a kid? Did he grow up a few miles away? Did he work for the train company? Did he bring the high school girls back here to screw?

Did he return every now and then to replay the night in question while he jacked off?

A black-and-white Magpie landed on a bush where it studied Wilde for a few seconds, then cawed and took off.

Sweat poured down his forehead.

It was every bit of a hundred right now.

This was the hottest summer he could remember for a long time.

He sat down on the ground on the shady side of the MG and leaned against the rear wheel. It felt good. The MG/TC was his baby, British Racing Green over tan leather, a two-seat roadster that only got made from 1946 to 1949. The English steering wheel was on the wrong side and it didn't have bumpers or a heater or a radio or hardly any other amenities, but it did have a drop top and a Moss Magnacharger engine. It also tended to make the women spread their legs ever so slightly when they sat in the passenger seat.

Women.

Wilde should be concentrating on the Raven case, but his thoughts turned to Neva, his mystery client from this morning.

Broken glass.

Broken glass to crawl over and smell her neck.

He needed to find her.

He needed to get into her life.

He needed to do it quickly.

She was the antidote to Night, who he'd fall back in love with, if he hadn't already.

When he got back to the office, Alabama was already back, dressed in blue shorts and a white blouse. Her legs were shapelier than Wilde expected and her arms were firm. Under different circumstances, he'd make a move on her.

"I've been thinking about something," he said. "The one thing we know for sure is that we're looking for someone who hates Raven enough to go to a lot of trouble to screw with him."

Alabama sat on top of the desk and dangled her legs.

"Okay."

"Now, the first go around, Raven was concentrating on his past cases to try to find who hated him."

"Right."

"Here's what I want you to do," Wilde said. "I want you to hit the gambling houses and whore houses and bars and find out if Raven has a secret side."

Alabama looked puzzled.

"Why?"

"If someone hates him, maybe it comes from that world and not from his detective world."

"That doesn't make sense," she said. "If that was the case, why wouldn't he just tell you about it?"

Wilde lit a cigarette.

"He wouldn't have been in a position to tell his own department members something like that the first go around," Wilde said. "I don't think he'd open up, just because it was me now instead of someone else. He'd want to delude himself into thinking that it was his detective life that drudged the killer up. So, get out there and find out if he has a secret life."

Alabama hopped off the desk.

"I'm going to need some seed money."

Wilde handed her a twenty, then thought about it and gave her a second one.

"Don't go overboard," he said. "Don't put your neck on the line. Just sniff around and report back to me."

"Okay."

She reached into a bag and pulled out a pair of white cotton panties.

"Thanks for this," she said. "I'll model it for you later."

Then she blew him a kiss and headed out the door.

23

Day One
July 15
Tuesday Evening

Nicole Wickliff showed up at Lloyd's building shortly after six, not looking anything like what Danton or Ying expected. She wasn't dressed up, anything but, in plain black pants and a simple white blouse, but she was hypnotic on a scale that rivaled Ying, if that was possible.

Long, dirty-blond hair.

Sensual.

Thirty.

Tall.

Taut.

She emerged from the hotel five minutes later, presumably with a gun, got into a cab that was waiting for her, and disappeared to the north—probably to her hotel.

"I had a weird thought," Ying said.

"How weird?"

"Pretty weird," she said. "Do you think she speaks English?"

Danton nodded.

"No one would send her if she didn't," he said. "She couldn't function."

"Why don't I try to get in good with her?" Ying said. "I could meet her by accident and buddy up to her. Maybe she has information we don't as to where Emmanuelle might be. If nothing else, at least I might be able to get a read as to when she'll strike."

Danton frowned.

"That's dangerous," he said.

Ying laughed.

"I can take care of myself," she said. "I thought you had that figured out by now."

"That's not what I'm talking about," Danton said. "What I'm talking about is you getting feelings for her. I might have to take her down, in fact I probably will have to take her down, we both know that. I don't want to have to second-guess your allegiance when that time comes."

"Trust me, my allegiance is with you."

"That's easy to say now. You haven't met her yet."

"Yeah, well—"

"French women can get a hold of you," he said. "They're not like American women. They're totally different. They can make you fall in love with them even if they're not trying and even if you don't want to."

"God, Danton, you're so paranoid," she said. "This is an infiltration mission, nothing more and nothing less."

He studied her.

"I promise," she added. "So, is that an okay I see in your eyes?"

He considered it.

"Okay."

She kissed him on the lips.

"Good," she said. "I want her to find me attractive. How should I dress?"

Danton looked at her.

"This isn't a game," he said. "If she figures out you're working against her, she'll slit your throat and never even blink. That's what she does. Don't ever forget it even for a second."

The words resonated.

Ying's face got serious.

Then she eased up and said, "You didn't answer my question. What should I wear?"

24

Day One
July 15
Tuesday Evening

The first thing Yardley did when she got back to her apartment was yank open the freezer door to make sure the scroll was still there, which it was. She pulled it out and stuck it under her pillow. So far the mystery client hadn't contacted either her or Taylor.

Maybe he was dead.

That wouldn't be good.

They needed him to find out where the scroll was discovered, if he knew, which he might not if he stole it from someone.

Her heart raced.

Slow down.

That's what she needed to do.

Slow down.

She was getting too intoxicated by the sudden appearance of hours that weren't mundane. She was riding an ancient wave in a way that had already twisted her. She was too convinced that this was her one and only chance at something special.

Her pact with Taylor was in place, at least verbally. Whether the woman would actually steal the scroll was yet to be determined.

They needed a foolproof charade.

That was the key.

They also needed to set it up without bringing a third person into the mix if possible.

The heat of the day was giving way to the thin Rocky Mountain air and dissipating more and more as the sun dipped lower. Yardley got a glass of wine, turned the radio to a blues station, crawled out the window and sat out on the fire escape.

Tomorrow would be a big day.

She shouldn't drink too much tonight.

The bottle was half gone when she thought she heard a noise from inside.

Faint.

Barely there.

But something.

It tingled her spine with the same tension she'd felt this morning in her office. She turned and looked in the window.

She saw nothing.

She heard nothing.

Then she crawled through the window, ever so quietly, while her blood raced.

25

Day One
July 15
Tuesday Night

The Bokaray was built for sin and seduction, with up-
holstered walls and ceilings, crystal chandeliers, a long
curved bar with a mirrored backdrop, countless ta-
bles, armless chairs, glass ashtrays and floral carpeting. Wilde
got there fifteen minutes before the show was set to start and
found the place already packed and resonating with a familiar
texture of cigarettes, perfume and liquor.

Nice.

It would be a good night.

Leigh Monroe was standing at the bar with a glass of wine
dangling in her hand, allowing a few of the more rich and relevant to get an up-close taste.

Ever the schmoozer.

Wilde headed over, wondering if he'd end up taking her
home tonight.

Time would tell.

With Leigh, you never knew.

She spotted him, broke out of her ring and intercepted him.

She put her arms around his neck, pressed her stomach to his and gave him a long loose kiss.

"Half the ladies are here tonight because the word got out about you being here," she said.

"I doubt that."

"Too bad they came in vain," she said. "You're mine tonight so be warned."

"Be warned yourself, I might call your bluff."

She rubbed her chest on him.

"Start calling, cowboy."

Life was best with a pair of drumsticks in hand, a right foot on the bass and a left on the cymbal. Music was a drug to listen to. It was ten times that when you were the one creating it, and twenty times that when a smoky packed club was busy getting lost in it.

Wilde's style was different.

He didn't stay in the background.

He didn't resign himself to a simple beat.

Instead he pounded and flailed and shook it up.

He laid in hooks.

He got loud.

He busted up the rhythm.

He led.

All the while he dangled a cigarette in his mouth.

He got drunk and let the liquor take over. That's when he was the best, when the sticks moved on their own.

The first set was good.

No, not good, Good.

Leigh's voice was pure sex.

During the break, something happened he didn't expect, namely Alabama showed up out of nowhere wearing a short blue dress, lots of cleavage and perfect legs encased in dangerous nylons. She put her arms around Wilde's neck, gave him a big sloppy kiss and said, "I found out something tonight about our client, the good detective Warner Raven."

"Oh, really—what?"

She nibbled on his lower lip.

"You were right about him."

"I was, was I?"

"Yes, you were," she said. "I already figured out my reward for doing such a good job."

"And what might that be?"

"Let's just say it involves you."

26

Day One
July 15
Tuesday Night

Sitting in her car down the street from the hitwoman's hotel, Ying realized that she should have dyed her hair, in case the $5-guy tipped the woman off about her and Danton.

Too late now.

Twilight came.

The lights turned on in the woman's room and every now and then a shadow moved behind the curtains.

Ying waited.

Patience.

That's what this game was about.

Patience.

A half hour after dark the woman emerged wearing high-heels and a sexy red dress with a black belt and got into a cab. Ying fired up the Packard and followed her to the Bokaray where the woman disappeared inside. Ying was underdressed in black pants and a blouse but came prepared. She pulled into an alley, moved over to the passenger side of the front seat, and changed into a tight black dress, nylons and black high heels. She found a place to park a block down and rolled ruby-red lipstick over her mouth as she walked towards the club.

Inside the place was packed.

She knew why.

Leigh Monroe was playing tonight.

What a coincidence that this is where she wanted to take Danton and now here she was. She looked around, didn't see the woman and headed for the bar, jamming through bodies and getting jammed in return. She ordered a white wine and then spotted her target, standing against the wall near the stage with a small glass in her hand, the kind that held hard liquor. Ying pulled a compact out of her purse, checked her face, then headed over.

She got next to her target as if by accident.

When the woman turned she said, "The band is good."

The woman looked into her eyes.

They darted away, then came back.

"Oui," she sad.

"Are you French?"

"Oui."

Ying smiled.

"I have a friend who knew a guy who knew another guy who wanted to go to France once," she said.

The woman smiled.

"That almost makes us best friends," she said.

"You think?"

The woman nodded, leaned into Ying's ear and said, "My name's Nicole."

"Ying."

As soon as Ying uttered the word she wanted to suck it back in. She should have used a fake.

"Ying?"

Ying nodded.

"I like it."

Ying looked around.

"I'm going to get drunk tonight," she said. "You want to join me?"

The woman clinked her glass against Ying's.

"Let's do it."

During the band's break, Nicole broke away and held a sidebar with the singer, Leigh Monroe. When the band started up for the second set, Leigh motioned Nicole on stage and told the crowd, "We have a special guest with us tonight from Paris."

Nicole took the microphone.

The band broke into Lady Day's "Ain't Nobody's Business."

Nicole sang in French.

By the time she stopped, everyone in the room was in love with her.

27

Day One
July 15
Tuesday Night

The noise Yardley heard inside her apartment turned out to be someone knocking on the door, which was strange because that hardly ever happened, especially this late. She didn't have a peephole so she made sure the chain was on properly and opened the door until it snagged.

Outside was a man, a man she had never seen before.

He was big, six-three at least, with a muscular jaw, a prominent nose and piercing eyes.

"I'm your client," the man said. "I'm here to pick up my package."

Yardley almost opened the door.

A recessed gene wouldn't let her.

"It's late and I'm heading to bed," she said. "We can meet in my office in the morning."

A crease developed between the man's eyes.

"Unfortunately there's been a change of plans about me retaining you." He took two fifty-dollar bills out of a wallet and held them at the opening. "That's for your troubles. Now, if you don't mind, I'd like to get my package and say goodnight."

Yardley swallowed.

"It's not here," she said.

"Where is it? Your office?"

"No, another lawyer has it."

"How could that be?"

"When the package got delivered, I was sitting with another lawyer at the time," she said. "We didn't know if the package was for me or her. She took possession of it."

A pause.

"Who is this other lawyer?"

Yardley looked at her watch.

"Look," she said. "I have to be in court first thing in the morning and need to get to bed. Come to my office at noon tomorrow and I'll have your package for you."

She expected the man to say *Fine* and head off.

Instead he stayed where he was.

"Did you open the package?"

"No."

"What about this other lawyer? Did she open it?"

She shrugged.

"I don't see why she would. What's your name, by the way?"

"That's not important," he said. "I'll be at your office at noon."

Then he left.

28

Day One
July 15
Tuesday Night

At the beginning of the second set, something happened that Wilde didn't expect, namely Leigh Monroe brought a woman on stage who sang "Ain't Nobody's Business" in French. At the end she turned around and looked directly into Wilde's eyes before stepping off stage.

His life shifted.

Just like that.

Two minutes later the cigarette fell out of his mouth and landed on the snare, then popped up wildly when the stick came down. It hung in the air directly above him and fell straight towards his head. He leaned back and caught it in his mouth.

A few people noticed.

One of them was the French woman.

She smiled and put her hands together in a silent clap.

Wilde nodded and looked as nonchalantly as he could, as if he did it a hundred times a night.

As soon as the set was over, he'd go over and find out who

she was. Not the minute it was over, he'd say hello to a few people first, just to keep her wondering. Then he'd meander over and appear to be surprised to find himself next to her all of a sudden.

His thoughts turned to what Alabama said during the break.

What she'd found out was that the detective, Warner Raven, had been in a camera club. Wilde himself had never been in one but everyone in the world knew how they worked. Pornography was technically illegal. So men formed camera clubs where they would hire a woman to pose nude while they clicked away. That wasn't pornography in the eyes of the law; it was art, protected by the First Amendment. The beauty of the club was that the men could pose the women in whatever postures they wanted and they could also do fetish photography like bondage and spanking and wrestling.

Raven had been in a club.

It was a little sleazy, a little dirty, and a little secret, but in the end didn't mean much. What Wilde found more interesting was that Raven stopped going to the club right around the time he got the first death threat.

It was too big of a coincidence to not mean something.

"Dig into it further," he told Alabama.

"Sure," she said. "Where do I sleep tonight?"

When the set ended Wilde headed straight for the French woman who was at the bar with a seriously attractive Asian woman. He had one thought and one thought only, namely to get her alone in a dark room and peel her clothes off one beautiful layer at a time.

Make her nasty.

Make her scream in French.

Make her hate him for what he was able to do to her.

29

Day One
July 15
Tuesday Night

The band's drummer walked over during the break with predator eyes but they weren't for Ying, they were for the French woman—Nicole. Ying watched as the two got very touchy very fast. Within minutes Ying was officially a third wheel.

"You kids have fun," she said.

Nicole grabbed her hand and said, "Wait. Don't go. Stay with me until after the show. Then we'll all go back to my hotel, all three of us. Okay?"

Wilde looked at Ying.

"I'm game."

Ying looked at him.

Then back at Nicole.

Then back at Wilde.

"What the hell," she said.

Nicole kissed her on the lips.

"It's settled, then."

30

Day One
July 15
Tuesday Night

When the mysterious client left, Yardley did something she would have never guessed, namely threw on shoes and followed him down the street in the shadows.

The wine made her brain spin.

It also kept her more in the open than she wanted.

Luckily the man didn't have a clue.

He never turned around.

Not once.

He walked briskly for two blocks, stepped into a phone booth and made a call. Yardley looked for a way to sneak up to hear the conversation but it was impossible.

When the man hung up, he didn't head down the street.

Instead he lit a cigarette and leaned against the booth.

Five minutes passed.

Then more minutes.

Suddenly a cab pulled up and the man hopped in.

Yardley stepped farther back into the shadows as the vehicle went past.

Another person was in the backseat, already facing the man and talking animatedly to him.

The person was a female.

Other than that, Yardley couldn't make her out.

DAY TWO

July 16
Wednesday

31

Day Two
July 16
Wednesday Morning

The French woman, Nicole, would have been the antidote to Night if she was in town to stay, but she wasn't, so Wilde reigned in his memories of the threesome last night and refused to let it morph into anything deeper.

Night.

Night.

Night.

Damn her to hell.

As soon as Wilde got himself functioning Wednesday morning, he headed straight to her house, parking in the alley and rapping on the back door.

It opened.

A woman stood there.

She wasn't Night.

She was a dark exotic thing. For some reason, he pictured her strolling on Mediterranean beaches in the day and breaking men's hearts at night.

"Is Night here?"

"No."

That was it.

No.

The woman said nothing else.

He'd been dismissed.

"Tell her Bryson stopped by," he said.

"I will."

The door closed.

Wilde hopped in the MG and headed for the office, wondering if the woman was some kind of black market trader in town to buy Grace Somerfield's stuff from Night.

Strange.

Alabama handed him a fresh cup of coffee as soon as he walked through the door, before he could even take his hat off and throw it at the rack.

"I did something bad," she said.

Wilde winced.

This wouldn't be pretty.

He could already tell.

"Like what?"

"I slept on your couch last night, like you told me to, while you so rudely went off with those other two women to do whatever it is you did," she said. "Anyway, it wasn't very comfy, the couch I mean, so I went out this morning and bought a futon. It's going to be delivered this afternoon."

"Last night was just a one night deal," he said "It was just a temporary thing to get you out of the Metropolitan until we can find you someplace decent."

She shrugged.

"It's too late now," she said. "I already moved in."

"You can't do that."

"My stuff's already in the closet," she said. "My toothbrush is already on the sink. I already put the toilet seat down and got a duplicate key made. Things like that can't be reversed so just get used to it."

Wilde took a sip of coffee.

"You put the toilet seat down?"

She smiled.

"Yes."

"That's just wrong," he said.

"Get used to it," she said. "It's the new look. Oh, I almost forgot to tell you, your little killer friend Night stopped by about ten minutes ago and picked up her bag of goodies."

Fine.

He was glad they were gone.

"Did she ask about me?"

"Not really," Alabama said. "She said *Thanks* when I gave her the bag, but that was about it." A pause then, "What do you see in her, Wilde, other than the fact that she's stunning?"

He pulled a book of matches out of his shirt pocket, set it on fire and looked at Alabama through the flames before tossing it in the ashtray. "We have history."

"How far back?"

"Too far," he said. "Eleventh grade."

"Was she your first?"

"First what?"

"First screw, first love, first broken heart, first everything."

He nodded.

"Yes."

"The first is the worst," Alabama said. "You never really get over the first."

Wilde tilted his head.

"You're exactly wrong," he said. "In fact, I've gotten over her three or four different times already."

She punched his arm.

"You're going to be hard to live with today, I can tell." A pause then, "So what do you want me to do today, stick with our detective friend Warner Raven?"

Wilde nodded.

"Stay with the sleaze angle," he said. "If he was in a camera club he was probably taking a hooker for a romp every now and then. Find out who; and find out what he whispered in her ear." He handed her two more twenties. "Here, take some tongue lubricant."

She stuffed it in her bra.

"What are you going to do while I'm doing all the work?"

He smiled.

Then the smile dropped off his face. "A woman's going to be abducted this week, probably today. She'll be killed on Friday. Just keep that in mind."

She shifted her feet.

"Give me more lubricant."

Wilde handed her three more twenties.

She stuffed them with the other two and headed for the door.

"Don't burn the place down while I'm gone."

32

Day Two
July 16
Wednesday Morning

D anton was disappointed that Ying never came back home last night to give him drunk sex, but he was glad for the reason, namely that she infiltrated Nicole to the point of even ending up with a threesome with her and a guy named Bryson Wilde.

"This guy, Bryson Wilde, was the drummer in the band," Ying said. "It turns out, though, that drumming is just a night gig he does every now and then. In the daytime he's actually a private investigator."

"Really?"

Ying nodded.

"Here's the important part," she said. "When Nicole found out he was a PI, she asked him if he'd do a project for her, for pay. Wilde said, *What kind of project?* At that point, Nicole pulled a photograph of Emmanuelle out of her suitcase and said, *I'm trying to find this woman.* Wilde asked, *Why?* Nicole said, *There's someone in town who's going to kill her. The reason I came here is to make sure that doesn't happen.*"

Danton's heart raced.

"She's lying," he said. "I hope you understand that."

"I do," Ying said.

"She's not here to protect anyone," he said. "She's here to kill her. The reason she said what she said is that after she kills her, Wilde will just think that she failed in her efforts to protect the woman. It would look too strange if she simply hired Wilde to find the woman and then the next day the woman turns up dead."

"I know that."

Danton paced.

"It's ironic that me and Nicole are saying the same thing," he said. "Deep down you have to be wondering which one of us is lying."

"I know who's lying," Ying said. "And it certainly wasn't the person who got Spencer out of my life."

"I hope you actually believe that," Danton said.

She grabbed his hand and pulled him towards the bedroom.

"Let me show you," she said.

Danton fell into step. As he unbuttoned Ying's blouse he said, "Did Wilde take the job?"

"Yes."

"Good," he said. "You're in tight with both of them. Keep your ear to the ground."

33

Day Two
July 16
Wednesday Morning

The client who knocked at the door last night was a fake, Yardley was almost positive of that. What she couldn't figure out was who the mysterious woman in the back of the cab was, the one pulling the strings. Yardley was aware of only two females who knew about the scroll and the fact that it came in a box from a mysterious client, namely Taylor Lee and Blanche Twister.

Was one of them double-crossing her?

Yardley twisted and shifted all night trying to figure it out.

By the time morning rolled around her groggy brain knew one thing and one thing only, she absolutely had to get the scroll someplace safe.

Her office didn't qualify.

Her apartment didn't qualify.

So, where?

Early morning at the break of dawn, she jogged down to her office, jimmied the door open with a screwdriver and then trashed the place.

She went home, wrapped a towel around her fist, went out onto the fire escape and then broke the window with a quick punch. The glass fell inside, as it would if there had been a break-in.

She then trashed the place.

There.

Done.

She rented a car and drove north looking for the perfect spot. Next to her on the seat was the scroll, tucked in a pillowcase. On the passenger side floorboard was the best digging device she could find in her apartment, an ice cream scooper.

The traffic thinned.

Then it disappeared almost entirely.

She came to a railroad crossing. A dirt service road ran parallel to the tracks. She looked around, saw no cars and turned the wheel to the right. The topography along the tracks was typical Colorado prairie, covered with rabbit brush, yucca and wild grass. She would have preferred more trees but the total lack of life and increasing remoteness offset it. She drove slowly, not wanting to throw up a rooster tail.

A couple of miles in, something appeared on the side, wedged into a bush.

She slowed as she came to it.

It was a body.

A man's body.

She stopped next to it.

He'd been beaten to death.

His eyes were open.

Ants crawled on his face.

She left the engine running, got out and looked around. A couple of magpies jumped off a bush in the distance and flew away. Something small rustled a few steps over to the right, but when she looked over it wasn't visible.

Probably a rabbit or a snake.

Against her better judgment she went through the man's pockets and found a wallet with a driver's license for one Michael Spencer and a folded sheet of paper that contained several handwritten names and telephone numbers. In his front pocket she found a key ring with 6 keys, plus a money clip with a lot of bills, not small ones either, the one showing on the outside was a twenty.

She pulled the bills out and counted the money.

There was over five hundred dollars.

The air was still and quiet.

No one was around, not anywhere.

She tossed the wallet, keys and money clip on the front seat and kept driving. About two hundred yards down the road she came upon a scraggly weather-beaten pinion pine about eight feet tall.

That would be a good marker.

She stopped next to it, killed the engine and stepped out.

No sounds or movement came from any direction.

She started at the pine and walked directly away from the road. At step twenty-two, she came to a moss rock the size of a basketball. She got down on all fours to see if she could move it, which she could. She buried the scroll one foot under where the rock had been and then moved the rock back into place. A little smoothing of the dirt hid any evidence of digging.

She got back into the car and drove for another three hundred yards, just so the turn marks, if there were any, wouldn't be by the pinion.

Then she turned around and headed back, wanting to go

fast but keeping her speed to where it wouldn't throw the dust too high.

She came across no one.

Not a single soul.

There.

Done.

On the drive back to the city she kept enough attention on the road to keep from smashing into anything, but most of her thoughts were on the body.

Michael Spencer.

What did he do to get himself murdered?

34

Day Two
July 16
Wednesday Morning

What was that woman's name? The one who ended up dead when Raven didn't follow orders? Wilde checked his notes. Jessica Dent. As soon as he read it he remembered. She's the one who got *Next time follow directions* carved into her body.

How did the killer pick her out?

Since it worked so well last time, would he do it the same way again?

Jessica Dent.

Jessica Dent.

Wilde pulled last year's phone book out of his bottom desk drawer to see if she was in there.

She was.

He grabbed his hat, tilted it over his left eye, lit a cigarette and headed for the street. On the way down the stairs he ran into the last person he expected, Nicole, one-third of last night's threesome.

"Where you going?" she asked.

"To do some snooping around."

"On my case?"

He winced.

"Actually a different one."

"Can I go with you?"

"It's not going to be anything exciting," he said.

She linked her arm through his.

"I'll be the judge of that."

She helped him drop the MG's top and said getting in, "What's our mission?"

"A woman got abducted and murdered fourteen months ago," Wilde said. "I want to find out where she got taken from, meaning the physical spot in the universe."

"Why?"

"Because the same man who took her is going to take another woman, probably today. I wouldn't mind being there at that physical point when he does it."

"You're kidding, right?"

"About which part?"

"All of it."

No.

He wasn't.

"The woman who gets taken today is going to die on Friday," he said.

Jessica Dent's phone book address was for a nice house on Grant Street, too nice, actually. Wilde rapped on the door and a middle-aged woman in a bathrobe and curlers answered.

"A woman named Jessica Dent used to live here," Wilde said. "I'm trying to find out what I can about her."

"Why?"

"I'm a private investigator," he said.

The woman studied him, deciding, then let him in.

A half hour later he left with some interesting information. The house had been a rental for at least ten years. Jessica was a renter. "But that was impossible because she was only a waitress," the woman said.

"Are you sure?"

She was.

"She worked at the Silver Spoon," the woman said. "I've seen her there myself. She even waited on me a few times. What a coincidence, huh?"

"Indeed."

Wilde also left with a suitcase that the woman discovered in the basement last month. "There's not much in there," she said, "just some clothes and papers and photos. I don't want it here, so if you find a home for it that would be great. It gives me the creeps to tell you the truth."

"I understand."

"She must have had a sugar daddy," Nicole said outside.

"Could be. The next stop is the restaurant. Are you hungry?"

She was.

"Yet another coincidence," Wilde said. "They're starting to rule the world."

The Silver Spoon wasn't where it was supposed to be.

It took them ten minutes of wandering around and asking questions to figure out that it was now the bar they were standing in front of, Tipsy's.

They walked inside to see if anyone who worked there knew anything about the restaurant or Jessica Dent.

No one did.

"Do you know why?" Wilde asked.

No.

She didn't.

"Because that's how my life works."

The asphalt was heating up.

It would break a hundred again.

"Did she get taken after a work shift?"

Wilde shrugged.

"That's my guess."

"Did she have a car?"

"Unknown."

"Well, we didn't drive that far to get here," Nicole said. "Five blocks maybe. She probably would have walked home, don't you think? Maybe someone took her between here and there."

Wilde looked at her.

"I'm impressed."

They walked the route.

It was very public.

There were no dark alleys or menacing hiding places for someone to jump out of.

"Sorry," Nicole said. "I just wasted our time."

"Maybe not," Wilde said.

"What do you mean?"

"It means there were no really good spots for a random abduction," he said. "If it wasn't random then it must have been planned."

"You think she was targeted all along?"

"Could be," he said. "Let's head back to the office and see what's in the suitcase."

"I need food first," she said. "Food and iced tea. So feed

me, cowboy."

"Feed you?"

"Right, feed me."

"As in, I'm the one who's going to pay?"

She nodded.

"We're not going to split the bill or anything like that?"

"No, you're going to pay."

"Are you going to leave the tip at least?"

"No, you are."

Wilde put his hand on her stomach and moved it around.

"You don't feel hungry," he said.

"Feel again," she said.

35

Day Two
July 16
Wednesday Morning

While Ying canvassed more hotels to see if she could locate Emmanuelle Martin, Danton got a crazy idea and decided to act on it, right here, right now. He took a cab to Nicole Wickliff's hotel, walked up the stairs two at a time to her room and rapped on the door with a racing heart.

His plan was simple.

He was going to tell the woman that he knew who she was and knew she was in town to kill Emmanuelle. He was going to tell her that he'd never let that happen. He was going to tell her she had one hour to pack her bags and get out of town.

Rap, rap, rap.

No answer.

Danton turned the knob.

It was locked.

He headed back down, spotted a greasy spoon across the street and drank coffee with one eye on the hotel.

This was important.

123

It was worth waiting for.

The area was a study in motion.

Everyone was on the move, focused, scampering.

Danton's cup got empty. A middle-aged woman in an apron came over with a pot and filled it with a smile.

"Merci," he said.

The word startled her.

"Are you French?"

He nodded.

"Oui."

"I've never remembered so many foreigners being in town," she said. "There was a woman from Greece in here yesterday."

Danton didn't care but smiled as if he did.

"That's interesting."

"Isn't it?"

He drank two more cups of coffee, put a nice tip on the table and left.

From there he headed over to Larimer Street.

Halfway there he turned around and headed back. The waitress was still there. Danton ordered another cup of coffee and said, "So there was a Greek woman in here yesterday, huh?"

Yes.

True.

"We haven't had a foreigner in here for years," she said. "Now two in as many days."

"Tell me about her," Danton said. "What'd she look like?"

36

Day Two
July 16
Wednesday Morning

From the lobby of the Daniels & Fisher Tower, Yardley surprised Taylor Lee with a telephone call that she was in the building and they needed to talk. They ended up walking down 16th Street as Yardley recanted how the mystery client showed up at her apartment last night. She didn't mention following the man or seeing him in the back of a cab with a woman.

If Taylor turned out to be that woman, she already knew about the client showing up at Yardley's door. In turn, she'd expect Yardley to tell her about it.

That's why Yardley was here.

That and to try to get a vibe as to whether the cab woman was in fact Taylor.

So far, she saw no definitive signs one way or the other.

Taylor looked at her watch.

"He's coming to your office at noon?"

"Right."

"It's already 10:30."

"I'm about 99 percent sure he's a fake," Yardley said. "The only person who knew that I had the scroll and got it from a mysterious client I'd never met is the woman I talked with at the university, Blanche Twister."

"You think she's behind this?"

Yardley shrugged.

"If she's not, then the client's real," Yardley said. "The way he had it dropped off so mysteriously and then showed up wanting it back without actually wanting any legal representation would force me to conclude he was just using me as a safe haven, which in turn meant he stole it. So, either way, I'm not going to give it to him."

"We need to think," Taylor said. "Where's the scroll right now?"

"In my freezer."

"Let's head over," Taylor said. "I'll take it and keep it safe until we can learn more about what's going on."

"Good idea."

When they got to Yardley's apartment, it was trashed and the freezer door was open.

The scroll was gone.

Gone.

Gone.

Gone.

Taylor hung her head and said, "This could be my fault. I told someone about the scroll."

"Who?"

37

Day Two
July 16
Wednesday Morning

Back at the office Wilde tossed his hat at the rack and missed. Nicole picked it up, walked back to where Wilde was and tossed it—bingo. "Beginner's luck." He opened the windows and got the fans blowing while Nicole looked around and said, "You're a man who believes in keeping the overhead low."

Wilde lit a cigarette.

"That's a polite way to say the place is a dump."

Nicole smiled.

"What's back here?" she said, opening the door to the adjoining room.

The room had no windows.

She stepped inside and said, "Look what I found."

Wilde headed over.

"What?"

When he got inside, Nicole kicked the door closed and brought the space into darkness. She put Wilde's hands on her breasts and said, "Me."

Wilde dropped the cigarette to the floor and ground it out with his wingtip.

Then he took her.

Hard.

Like an animal.

Afterwards, getting dressed, Nicole said, "You were pretty rough."

"Sorry," he said.

She gave him a kiss.

"That wasn't a complaint."

He wrapped his arms around her.

"I wish you didn't have to go back to Paris."

Silence.

Then, "Maybe I won't."

Wilde's world shifted.

He could picture her in his life, not just short term but five or ten years from now. He was thirty-one. It wouldn't kill him to settle down, maybe even have a rug rat or two.

They opened Jessica Dent's suitcase. Inside was a black-and-white photograph of two women with their arms around each other. Me and Constance was handwritten on the back. Both women were pretty. There was no date.

"Which one is Jessica?"

Wilde studied the photo.

"The one who's not Constance," he said. "Did you mean it when you said you might not go back to Paris?"

Nicole walked to the window and looked down.

Then she turned and said, "To be honest, I think Denver's too small for me. I could be happy in New York though, if the right person was with me. Or Paris, of course. Have you ever been there?"

"No."

"You'd be amazed," she said.

"So what are you saying, that you want me to come to Paris?"

She nodded.

"I guess I am," she said. "You'd do fine there. You could even stay in the PI business."

Wilde tilted his head.

"Most of the reason I can make this work is because I know the lay of the land and have a network of people who will talk to me," he said. "I wouldn't have that in Paris."

"I'm not saying it wouldn't take time."

"I can't even speak French."

"You'd pick it up."

"You think?"

She nodded.

"Think about it," she said. "I will too, for that matter. Right now the only thing I know for certain is that I don't want to have to say goodbye to you."

Wilde lit a cigarette.

"You don't even know who I am."

"I know enough."

Lots of clothes were inside the suitcase. Wilde picked up the photo and pointed to the woman on the right. "That's Jessica Dent," he sad.

"How do you know?"

Wilde held up a blouse from the suitcase.

"Look familiar?"

It did.

The woman on the right was wearing it.

"Let's find Constance and talk to her," he said.

38

Day Two
July 16
Wednesday Morning

Late morning Ying called and said, "I'm at the Albany Hotel on 17th Street. A French woman checked in here yesterday under the name Monique Sanbeau."

Lightning shot through Danton's veins.

"Do you have a description of her?"

"No, just the name," Ying said. "There's a problem. I think Kent Dawson's on my tail."

"Why?"

"I'm not positive," she said. "I turned around about five minutes ago and a man who was facing me spun the other way and walked off. I didn't see his face but he was the size of Dawson and had his posture."

Danton paced.

"What's Dawson look like?"

She described him.

Big.

Strong.

Mean.

A scar on his forehead.

"The guy you saw, what's he wearing?"

"A suit."

"What color?"

"Dark blue."

"Is he wearing a hat?"

"Yes, brown."

A pause.

"Okay, do this," Danton said. "Stay where you are until exactly 10:30, then come out the front of the hotel and head down the sidewalk to the right. I'm going to be positioned across the street and see if someone follows you. Don't look around. I'll do all the looking. Do you understand?"

Yes.

She did.

Danton called a cab, got a twelve-minute ride, and took a window seat in a coffee shop a half block down 17th Street from the hotel.

At 10:32 Ying walked past on the opposite side of the street, looking straight ahead.

"Come on," Danton muttered. "Follow her."

Fifty steps later a man came into sight.

Dark blue suit.

Brown hat.

Danton waited until he passed, then crossed the street and followed twenty steps behind.

Ying turned right at the corner.

So did the blue suit.

So did Danton.

He closed the gap until he was right behind the man and said, "Hey, Dawson."

The man turned.

Danton wasn't prepared for what he saw.

The man was strong.

Intense.

No-nonsense.

Danton wasn't sure he could take him in a fair fight. If he could it would come with a lot of pain and damage. He put on his meanest face and said, "Get out of Ying's life, right now, this second, forever. If you even look at her again I'm going to kill you with my bare hands."

The man took a stance.

"Go ahead," he said. "Do it."

Danton leaned in until they were nose to nose.

"You've been warned," he said.

Then he walked away.

Five steps later he heard over his shoulder, "Hey, asshole."

He turned.

"Spencer sends his regards."

Danton almost said, *Heed the warning, it's your only one.*

He didn't though.

He'd already made his point.

He tipped his hat, then walked away.

Heartbeats later a python-strong arm grabbed him around the neck from behind and the point of a knife pinched into the small of his back.

"Do you like this? Huh, bitch?"

Danton struggled.

The knife went deeper.

"Be out of town by nightfall. Do you understand?"

The man kept him locked in position for a second.

Then another.

And another.

Suddenly the stranglehold on Danton's neck disappeared and an elbow crashed into his back.

He fell to the sidewalk.

"Nightfall," the man said.

39

Day Two
July 16
Wednesday Noon

Yardley's office had two windows, currently wide open, but they were both on the same wall and offered no cross-ventilation. She got down on her knees in front of the floor fan, unbuttoned her blouse and let the wind blow against her stomach.

It was ten minutes before noon.

The so-called "client" would be here shortly to claim the scroll. Yardley had the door locked, not yet sure if she'd answer when the knock came.

At two minutes before the hour, she buttoned her blouse and sat behind her desk.

A minute passed, then another.

No knock came.

The doorknob didn't jiggle.

The office was trashed. She hadn't moved a thing. It was proof to the client that someone has stolen the scroll.

She could think of nothing else, only the impending knock.

Another minute passed.

Her heart raced.

He was coming, any second now.

She braced herself.

Five minutes passed.

Then fifteen.

Then thirty.

She wiped sweat off her forehead.

Five more minutes passed.

She left the office, took the back stairwell down to the alley and walked aimlessly down Blake Street, having no destination, doing nothing more than feeding the need to be in motion while she tried to make sense of what was happening.

Maybe the client didn't show because he saw her bury the scroll this morning and had already dug it up and disappeared forever. While theoretically possible, it was equally improbable. Yardley would have heard or seen someone if they'd been around. No one could have kept up with her on the service road unless they were in a car. Clearly no car had been on the road. She would have felt the vibration, not to mention smell the dust.

Think.

Think.

Think.

Then a thought came to her, a thought that made her heart pound. Taylor Lee appeared to have fallen for the charade this morning that someone stole the scroll last night. If that was the case, Taylor would know that sending the client at noon would be fruitless and, if anything, might even lead to Yardley asking the right questions and figuring out that Taylor was pulling the strings.

That was it.

The client didn't show because Taylor Lee called him off, meaning she was the woman in the back of the cab last night. So what was she thinking at this point, that the man she hired to pose as a client double-crossed her and stole the scroll for his own?

Yardley turned and headed for the Daniels & Fisher Tower.

She needed to shadow Taylor.

40

Day Two
July 16
Wednesday Noon

Detective Warner Raven popped in shortly before noon while Nicole was out getting sandwiches. He handed Wilde a stack of manila folders and said, "This is the official file on Jessica Dent. As to all my other cases before that, they're going to be almost impossible to get out."

"I'll start here," Wilde said.

"How's it going so far?"

Wilde showed him the suitcase. "I'm beginning to think she was targeted rather than a random pick, based on the fact there was no good random spots to snatch her between where she worked as a waitress and her house. By the way, how'd she afford the rent on that place?"

Raven shook his head.

"We never figured that out," Raven said. "Personally I think she had a sugar daddy."

"Maybe Mr. Sugar killed her."

"I doubt it," Raven said. "The chance of her having a sugar

daddy who also hated me for some reason is infinitesimal."

"Infinitesimal?"

"Right."

"Raven, this is me, Wilde. Don't use big words. All you're going to do is make me spend all my time flipping through a Webster's."

Raven smiled.

"Has anyone disappeared yet?" Wilde asked.

"Not that I know of," Raven said. "Today's going to be the day though. I can feel it." He looked at his watch and stuck his hat back on. "I better run. Is there a back way out of here?"

Wilde opened the door and pointed down the hall.

"That'll dump you into the alley."

Nicole walked in fifteen minutes later with a ham sandwich and an RC Cola for Wilde, who was suddenly starved, and a salad for herself. Wilde took a giant bite and said, "This is the official police file on Jessica Dent. There's no mention of a Constance in here anywhere."

"You think they would have talked to her."

Wilde shrugged.

"Only if they knew about her," he said.

He pointed his face back into the file and flipped through it for the second time. Just as he washed the last bit of sandwich down with the last swallow of RC Cola, he noticed something.

"Hey, look at this," he said. "It's Jessica's day calendar. It says *Lunch with CB*. C might be Constance." He picked up last year's phonebook, handed it to Nicole and said, "Do me a favor and go through the Bs and see if you find a Constance B."

She looked at him in wonder.

"You expect me to go through every B?"

"No, go straight to the right one if you want," he said. "I

don't care."

She punched him on the arm.

"You're impossible to be around sometimes," she said. "You know that I hope."

"So I've heard."

"What are you going to be doing while I do the work?"

He stood up, walked to the window and looked out. Then he turned and said, "Looking out the window."

"Looking out the window?"

"Right, looking out the window, and thinking."

He set a book of matches on fire.

Then another.

He was reaching for a third when Nicole said, "Bingo. Constance Black."

"You're kidding, right?"

No.

She wasn't.

"This is so weird because I had a feeling her name was Black."

"Next time tell me that before I start looking."

"I didn't say I actually knew what it was, just that I had a feeling."

"Yeah, well, next time just tell, either way."

"Will do," he said.

He dialed the woman's number. It didn't ring.

"Out of service," he said. "Let's drive over to her address and see if she's home."

Nicole balked.

"When are we going to get to my case? It's just as important."

Wilde lit a cigarette and blew smoke.

"Let me work on this one until the end of the day," he said. "Then you own me until morning."

She fell into step. "Fair enough."

41

Day Two
July 16
Wednesday Afternoon

Danton was going to let Kent Dawson live so long as the man got out of Ying's life. That was before Dawson got all stupid and mean with the chokehold and knife. Now it was clear that Danton had no choice but to do what he had to do.

He'd do it tonight.

He'd do it with his bare fists or a blade.

Right now he wasn't interested in wasting too many brain cells on it.

He was a lot more interested in determining if the French woman who checked into the Albany Hotel under the name Monique Sanbeau was in fact Emmanuelle Martin.

He walked into the lobby and told the man at the registration desk, "Can you call up to Monique Sanbeau's room and tell her Jacques is here to see her."

The man dialed.

Danton watched the numbers, 301.

After eight rings the man hung up and said, "She's not answering."

Danton nodded.

"Thanks, I'll try back later."

He walked out the front into bright Colorado sunshine, then swung around to the rear and climbed up the exterior fire escape to the third floor. He knocked on 301—the first room inside—got no answer, tried the knob and found it locked.

Back on the fire escape, he noticed that the room's window was open—two meters away. He got to the outside of the fire escape, positioned himself and took a deep breath.

He didn't look down.

He looked only at the window.

Then he jumped.

His left hand hit the sill and fell off.

His right hand hit the sill and gripped it.

He hung with one arm, making sure his hold was solid, then twisted his body up and made his way in.

No one was in the room.

A suitcase was on the floor in the corner.

He swung it onto the bed and opened it.

What he saw he liked.

The clothes belonged to Emmanuelle.

Under the clothes was a bottle of perfume. He opened it and took a whiff. It smelled like Emmanuelle. He dabbed a drop on his neck, put everything back as he found it and left.

Outside, he took a position across the street.

Then he waited.

He'd stay right there no matter how long it took.

42

Day Two
July 16
Wednesday Afternoon

Yardley didn't have to wait long before something happened. Taylor busted out the bottom of the Daniels and Fisher Tower visibly upset and walked north at a frantic pace. Yardley followed as far back as she could without losing sight. After four blocks it became clear where the woman was headed—Yardley's office.

What the hell?

Yardley watched the woman disappear into her building, waited an appropriate time, then intercepted her in the stairway as she was coming down.

She put a surprised look on her face.

"Taylor."

The woman's face was tense.

Serious.

On the verge of tears.

"We need to talk," she said.

"Come on up."

Inside, the office was still trashed. Taylor looked around,

confused.

"He obviously came here before hitting my apartment," Yardley said.

"I'm in trouble," Taylor said. "Serious trouble."

"What do you mean?"

"The client showed up at my office a half hour ago."

"The client who came to see me, the big man?"

Taylor shook her head.

"No," she said. "He's big, over six feet, but he has long hair. He speaks English but he's Greek, he has a strong Greek accent. He showed up out of the blue to meet with me. The reason he wanted to hire me was to process the custom and export papers to get the scroll out of the United States and into Greece. When I told him about what happened to the scroll—how another lawyer was at the table when it got delivered and how she took it and then it got stolen—he got very quiet. Then he said, *Get it back. Get it back now.* He gave me the coldest look I've ever seen." A pause, then, "He's going to kill me if I don't get it back."

"Did he actually say that?"

"No," Taylor said. "It was in his eyes though. It was so real that it filled the room and rolled right up my spine."

"Did you tell him who the other lawyer was?"

"Unfortunately, yes," Taylor said.

"You told him my name?"

"That was earlier in the conversation before I realized how he was going to react," Taylor said. "I was just going with the truth. I'm sorry."

Yardley stood up and looked out the window.

Then she turned and said, "So what do we do?

"We need to get the scroll back. If we don't, I'm going to end up dead. Maybe you too."

Yardley said nothing.

"He's going to want to interrogate you," Taylor added. "I came over here as fast as I could to warn you. We should leave. Right now."

43

Day Two
July 16
Wednesday Afternoon

Constance Black's address turned out to be the Overview Apartments on Lincoln Street. Wilde ran an index finger down the buzzers, didn't see her name and pressed *Manager*. A middle-aged man came down the hall wiping his hands on dirty corduroy pants.

"You the ones who buzzed me?"

Yes.

They were looking for Constance Black.

"Constance Black," the man repeated. "Can't say that rings a bell."

Wilde pulled a photo out of his pocket, pointed to the woman on the left and said, "That's her."

The man studied it for a heartbeat and smiled.

"Right," he said. "Connie. I haven't thought about her since she took off. That was—what?—a year or two ago."

"Where'd she go? Do you have a forwarding address?"

No.

He didn't.

"It was the strangest thing," the man said. "One day she came running down the steps. It looked like something was wrong so I said, *Are you okay?* She said, *I'm out of here and I won't be back.* That was the honest to God truth too. That was the last time I saw her. The strange thing is, she left everything in her apartment. I mean everything—dishes, food, furniture, 33s, clothes, everything."

"That's weird," Wilde said.

"She just up and left. I had some other vacancies at the time so I just let everything sit in her apartment for a while in case she showed back up," he said. "After three months or so she still hadn't come back so I cleaned everything out. Most of it I gave to charity. She never did come back even to this day."

Wilde scratched his head.

"Can you give me a better idea when this happened?"

The man retreated in thought.

"Not from memory," he said. "It was more than a year ago. I'd have to check the paperwork if you need something more accurate than that."

At Wilde's request, the man checked it.

Constance Black left fourteen months ago on a Tuesday.

It was the same Tuesday that detective Warner Raven got his death threat, *You will die on Friday.*

It was the day before Jessica Dent got abducted.

Back at the MG Nicole said, "Constance Black knew what was coming. If we can find her we'll have the key."

Wilde frowned.

"She's dead. She ran but she didn't make it."

"How do you know?"

"She never came back for anything."

"Obviously something scared her out of her wits," Nicole

said. "Maybe it scared her so bad that she just headed to another state."

"Maybe," Wilde said, "but if you asked me to bet a dollar
on it one way or the other, I'd lay my money down on her being
dead."

"You can't be sure."

"Put yourself in her shoes," he said. "If you made it to
another state and were safe and sound, what would you do?
You'd call a friend and ask them to slip into your apartment
one night and get your stuff—your clothes and records, at a
minimum. That didn't happen. The reason it didn't happen is
because the phone call never happened." A pause then, "She's
dead. Trust me."

Nicole exhaled.

"Suppose you're right, now what?"

Wilde looked into the distance.

Then he cranked over the engine and said, "Now we go to
plan B."

"What's plan B?"

Wilde shifted into first, waited for a clear spot and pulled
out.

"It's a place I was hoping I wouldn't have to go."

44

Day Two
July 16
Wednesday Afternoon

Danton waited patiently for Emmanuelle to return to the Albany. Half an hour passed, then an hour, and his patience thinned. After two hours he was pacing and pissed, almost at the breaking point. He held out for thirty more minutes and then headed into the hotel and took the stairs to the third floor, on the chance that Emmanuelle had come in the back way.

He knocked.

No one answered.

He bounded down the stairs two at a time and headed straight for the man at the front desk.

"I'm back to see if Monique has returned yet," he said.

"She hasn't," the man said. "But she called to see if anyone had left any messages and I gave her your message."

Message.

What message?

Danton hadn't left a message.

"What message?"

"That you'd stopped by to see her," the man said.

"What'd she say?"

"She asked me to describe you."

Damn it!

Danton's instinct was to smash his fist on the counter. Instead he took a deep breath, said "Thanks," and walked away.

Damn it!

Damn it!

Damn it to hell!

She'd never come back.

She'd abandon everything in place.

She'd change her name and go even deeper.

He'd lost her.

45

Day Two
July 16
Wednesday Afternoon

The scroll had a hold on Yardley. She knew that before on an unconscious level but now it smacked her in the face with the force of a two-by-four. She didn't tell Taylor that it was actually in her possession, safe and sound, available to be dug up and handed over to the client.

Taylor was in danger.

Yardley could bring that danger to a screeching halt.

Still, she hesitated.

The client would need to prove the scroll was his and that he got it through legitimate means. If and when that happened, Yardley would decide whether to turn it over. It was the most important thing to ever come into her life.

It made her someone.

It elevated her mundane life to a new level.

She didn't want that to end.

It was wrong but that's the way it was.

She needed to do two things short-term. First, watch Taylor's back so nothing happened to her. Second, get interrogated by the client to find out if he was dangerous and where his alleged ownership rights came from.

"I have to get back to work," Taylor said. "Stop by at the end of the day and we'll figure out how to handle tonight."

"Will do."

"In the meantime stay away from your apartment and your office," Taylor added.

"Will do."

"I'm serious."

"I understand."

When Taylor left, Yardley headed back to the office. If she was going to be interrogated, it might as well be sooner than later.

She locked the door and paced.

Thirty minutes passed.

Nothing happened.

Her thoughts turned to the dead man by the railroad tracks, Michael Spencer. She looked him up in the phone book and found he lived on Clarkson east of Colfax. She had the rental car until tomorrow morning. It would be easy to head over there. One of the keys on the chain probably fit his door.

Should she go over and take a peek around?

The piece of paper from Spencer's wallet, the one with a list of names and phone numbers, was a mystery. Maybe one of those names belonged to Spencer's killer. But if it did, why would he leave it there?

Maybe it was a fake.

Maybe he put it there to misdirect the police.

Interesting.

Maybe she should at least drive down the street and see what the man's house looked like.

That would be better than sitting in a hot office.

She threw Spencer's wallet and keys in her purse, locked the office and headed down the stairs.

46

Day Two
July 16
Wednesday Afternoon

Wilde knew he was stretching the bounds of professionalism by letting Nicole tag along on the investigation of another client's case, but he wouldn't be able to think if she wasn't around. He wanted her by his side, every minute, every step. He needed to figure out if it was true that they might actually end up together, in New York or Paris or wherever.

They didn't talk much on the drive back to the office, thanks to the noise of the wind and the engine.

Inside, he tossed his hat at the rack.

It hit the edge, almost snagged but then dropped to the floor.

"You're getting closer," Nicole said.

She picked it, went back to where Wilde was and said, "It's all in the wrist. Watch carefully."

She flung the hat.

It hit and stuck.

"See?"

Wilde shook his head and lit a cigarette.

"Jessica Dent wasn't a random pick," he said. "I'm more convinced of that than even before, now that we know she was friends with Constance Black who got killed—or at a minimum got scared to death and left town—almost on the same day. Something was going on, something more complicated than Raven knew about, assuming he's innocent."

Nicole raised an eyebrow.

"Assuming he's innocent?"

Wilde nodded.

"What's that supposed to mean, exactly?"

Wilde blew smoke.

"I'm starting to think that he might be the one who killed Jessica Dent."

"You're kidding, right?"

Wilde lit a book of matches on fire and let the flames burn down to his fingertips. Then he looked out the window, saw no one below and tossed it down to the sidewalk.

"What I'm thinking," he said, "is that the whole phone call he allegedly got—*You will die on Friday*—was a charade. It was a misdirect, something like a magician would do."

"I'm not following."

"Okay, put yourself in his shoes for a moment and assume, just for the sake of argument, that he wants to kill Jessica Dent for some reason," Wilde said. "What he does is tell everyone he got this weird phone call about getting killed on Friday. That makes it seem like there's some maniac out there. Low and behold, a body shows up on Friday. All the evidence points directly at the maniac as the killer. At the same time it points directly away from Raven. He's created his own alibi."

Nicole chewed on it.

"That's quite a theory," she said, "but that's all it is. It's speculation piled on speculation piled on speculation. It's a mountain of speculation."

Wilde nodded.

"True," he said, "but that's what my gut's telling me."

"Your gut's not a brain though, is it?"

Wilde laughed.

"I don't think so."

"Well, keep that in mind."

"My gut is a gut though," he said. "It's got those gut feelings that my brain doesn't."

"So what are you going to do? Investigate Raven as if he was the murderer?"

Wilde nodded.

"I don't have a choice."

"That's dangerous."

"I understand."

"If he is the murderer and finds out you're sneaking around in his shadows ... well ... you know."

Right.

He knew.

He knew all too well.

"You also need to consider something else," Nicole said. "You could be totally wrong about him. Jessica Dent might have gone down exactly the way he said. If that's the case, you'll be wasting what little time you have."

"It's a risk I'm going to have to take," he said. "I'm going to stake him out tonight."

"Why?"

"To see if he abducts a woman."

"Can I come along?"

Wilde shook his head.

"Negative. It's too dangerous."

She walked over, put her arms around his neck and whispered in his ear, "Are you sure?"

"Yes."

She brought her lips dangerously close to his.

"How about now? Are you still sure?"

"Yes."

She kissed him.

"How about now?"

"Yes."

She kissed him again.

"Earlier you said I owned you tonight," she said. "Were you telling the truth?"

Damn it.

He was trapped.

"Yes," he said.

"Then I guess it looks like I'm going with you."

"I guess you are."

She kissed him one more time and then pulled back. "If you're right about Raven, why would he hire you?"

"To further perpetuate the illusion," Wilde said. "Before it's all over, he'll leak it to the people in the department that he hired me. He's a clever guy."

"That's more speculation," Nicole said. "I'd think just the opposite, namely that if he killed Jessica, the last thing he'd do is get a PI involved."

"That's true if he thought the PI would succeed," Wilde said.

"What are you saying, that he hired you because he didn't think you were smart enough to figure it out?"

Wilde nodded.

"He hired me to fail."

Nicole wasn't impressed.

"We'll see if anything materializes tonight," she said. "If it doesn't, I think you should get back on track."

47

Day Two
July 16
Wednesday Afternoon

Danton wandered the streets of Denver, ready to snap for having gotten so close to finding Emmanuelle and then losing her.

Stupid.

That's what he was.

Beyond stupid.

He should never have talked to the registration desk. He should have just waited outside until Emmanuelle showed up. That's all he had to do.

Why didn't he do that?

Why didn't he just be patient?

Suddenly a thought came to him, a thought that made him head back to the hotel as fast as his feet would go. The man behind the desk was still there.

Danton said, "I'd like to leave a message for Monique Sanbeau."

The man nodded.

Sure.

No problem.

Danton spotted a piece of paper and scribbled on it—DD, followed by Ying's phone number. Emmanuelle would recognize DD as Degare Danton. Even though she believed he was in town to kill her, she'd probably feel safe enough to call, if for no other reason than to feel him out.

"Tell her to call DD at this number," he said.

The man put the paper in the wall slot marked 301.

"Done," he said. "Anything else."

"Just tell her it's important."

"I will."

Danton took a cab back to Ying's. She wasn't home but had left the key under the mat. He stayed in the living room, pacing next to the phone and willing it to ring.

Ten minutes later it did.

He took a deep breath and answered.

It wasn't Emmanuelle.

It was Kent Dawson. "I don't see you leaving town. Do you think I was joking with you?"

Danton smashed his fist into the wall.

It bounced off a stud without breaking the plaster.

"Come on over right now," he said. "I'm waiting for you. Let's do it."

Silence.

Then the line went dead.

48

Day Two
July 16
Wednesday Afternoon

Michael Spencer's house was a large stone stand-alone of prominence and architectural interest on the east edge of Capitol Hill. Yardley walked past it once on the opposite side of the street, to all intents and purposes paying no attention. Fifteen minutes later she doubled back, walked up to the front door and tried the keys from Spencer's pocket.

The third one worked.

She pushed the door open halfway and stuck her head through.

"Anyone home?"

No answer.

"Hello?"

Silence.

She stepped inside, shut the door and listened for sounds or vibrations. The air was coffin-quiet. She almost turned around and left but instead took one step at a time deeper into the guts of the structure.

"Okay, Michael Spencer. Tell me why you're dead."

There were no signs of a struggle or violence or blood.

He hadn't been killed here.

The house hadn't been ransacked.

She found nothing of interest on the first floor and headed up a winding staircase. Suddenly a door slammed down below. Someone was in the house.

Hide.

Hide.

Hide.

She tiptoed into the bathroom, stepped into the tub and closed the shower curtain. A squeak came from the rod, barely perceptible but perceptible nonetheless.

She held her breath.

A cough sounded.

It was deep.

Throaty.

It belonged to a man.

49

Day Two
July 16
Wednesday Afternoon

The bricks and asphalt of Larimer Street soaked up every possible ray of sun and relentlessly flung them at every person, animal and insect that was unfortunate enough to be within flinging distance. Wilde wiped sweat off his brow and pictured a cold iced tea sliding down his throat as he flipped through the phone book for an address.

He grabbed his hat from the rack, dipped it over his left eye and said, "Let's take a field trip."

Nicole fell into step.

"Where we going?"

"Someplace we shouldn't."

"As in where?"

"We're going to stake out Warner Raven's place tonight, remember?"

Yes.

She remembered.

"It's not exactly night yet."

"I've never seen the place," Wilde said. "I want to drive by and get my bearings."

Raven, it turned out, lived in a nice standalone house on the east side near Colorado Boulevard. The houses had driveways meaning street parking wasn't as big a problem as inner-city Denver. A drive-by showed the curtains closed but the windows open six inches or so.

Wilde parked a block over and looked at Nicole.

"I'm half tempted to go in," he said.

"You're kidding, right?"

He wasn't.

Not in the least.

"It's the quickest way to figure out if I'm on track or not," he said. "If you're right and Raven's a misdirect, I'd rather know it now than later."

Nicole chewed on it.

"I'm coming with you."

Wilde stepped out of the car.

"Just wait here, I'll be right back."

He headed for the house.

Ten steps later he found Nicole at his side.

"You forgot something," she said.

"What?"

"Me."

"You just do whatever you want, don't you?"

"Pretty much, so get used to it."

They headed up the driveway as if they owned the place, then swung to the back and entered through a bedroom window.

There.

Done deal.

Wilde peeked around to see if any nosy neighbors were craning their necks to get a better look at what just happened.

He saw no one.

"Don't touch anything."

"Okay."

"I'm serious."

"I said okay."

Wilde slapped her ass.

"Say it in French."

"Oui."

"That's better," he said. "And stop trying to feel my hand with your ass. It's not polite."

She smiled.

"Sorry."

Wilde slapped it again.

"Hey, we just talked about that."

"I guess it just can't help itself," she said. "What are we looking for exactly?"

"The usual stuff," Wilde said. "Bloody heads hanging from meat hooks, the stench of a thousand rotting corpses, that kind of thing. You'll know it when you see it."

50

Day Two
July 16
Wednesday Afternoon

anton was pacing next to the phone when it rang and the voice of none other than Emmanuelle came through. "I'm sorry I tried to kill you," she said in French.

"I have to admit, it was a bit of a shocker," he said. "We need to get together and talk."

"I can't."

"Why not?"

"Because I'm not sure what you'll do to me."

"I'm not going to hurt you."

"There's no way I can be sure of that," she said. "Not at this point."

"Let me show my good faith by sharing some news with you," he said "There's a French woman in town looking to kill you." With that, he told her about the woman going under the name Nicole Wickliff, how he broke into her hotel room and found pictures of Emmanuelle.

"Where is she staying?"

Danton told her adding, "Room 301. There's an exterior fire escape that comes pretty close to her room window."

"What's she look like?" Emmanuelle asked.

"Sexy."

Silence.

"Blond, dirty."

Then, "Thanks."

The line went dead.

Two minutes later the phone rang again. Danton thought it was Emmanuelle with something on her mind but it turned out to be Ying calling from a payphone.

"I just swung by Spencer's house, to see if the cops were there by any chance," she said. "Guess whose car was parked in the driveway?"

Danton didn't know.

"Kent Dawson's."

Dawson.

The asshole.

"What's he doing there?"

"My guess is that the dirt they have on me is being kept at Spencer's place. Dawson knows that Spencer's body will show up sooner or later and the cops will end up over there snooping around," she said. "He wants to get the dirt while it's there to get. That way he can keep his hooks in me."

Danton clenched his hand.

"Swing over and get me."

"Why?"

"Because it's time for Dawson to decide if he wants to live or not."

Silence.

Then, "I'll be there in five minutes."

51

Day Two
July 16
Wednesday Afternoon

When Yardley dared to peek around the edge of the shower curtain, she could see into the bedroom thanks to the reflection of the mirror above the sink. Based on the sounds from downstairs, the man was an intruder, working fast, rustling through things.

He was probably the one who killed Spencer.

Five minutes into the search, he stopped to make a telephone call. *I don't see you leaving town. Do you think I was joking with you?* A few heartbeats later he threw the phone against the wall and shouted, *You're dead, Danton. Deader than dead. I should have just done it this afternoon.*

Yardley memorized the name—*Danton.*

Danton.

Danton.

Vibrations came from the stairway.

The man was heading closer.

Yardley couldn't breathe.

Lightning pumped through her veins.

In three heartbeats a hand would grab the curtain and rip it back.

She could feel it.

It was coming.

The end of her life was here.

She wanted to peek out.

She wanted to see his face.

Instead she got her body as still as she could. She didn't move her arms or legs or hands. She didn't shift her feet. She breathed through a quiet open mouth. Sooner or later a part of her body would move. She couldn't stay like this forever.

The man came into the bedroom.

Drawers opened.

The contents got dumped to the floor.

The man shifted them around with his foot, looking for whatever it was he was looking for.

His breathing was heavy.

He smashed the wall with his fist.

Then he suddenly got coffin-quiet and tiptoed towards the hall.

Noises came from downstairs.

Someone else was in the house.

The man swore under his breath, then opened a bedroom window and jumped out.

Yardley ran to the window and looked down.

The man was big, strong and mean.

Suddenly he looked up.

Straight up.

Directly into her eyes.

He had a cleft chin and a scar on his forehead.

He paused for a moment as if deciding whether to come back, then he turned and ran.

A shout came from downstairs.

"Dawson!"

Silence.

"Dawson!"

No answer.

Yardley gauged the distance to the ground. It was a long way but probably wouldn't kill her. She got her body through, took a deep breath and realized she couldn't do it.

It was too far.

Suddenly she lost her balance and fell.

52

Day Two
July 16
Wednesday Afternoon

Raven's house was hotter than hot. The windows might have been cracked to keep the place from turning into a complete oven, but that was about it. Three or four fans were blowing at full force, not doing anything other than moving fiery air from one part of the house to another. Wilde stood in front of one of them as he looked around. He lifted his hat and wiped the sweat off his forehead with the back of his hand.

"What I'm primarily interested in is seeing if there's anything that connects Raven to either Jessica Dent or Constance Black," he said. "That will probably take the shape of either papers or photographs."

"Okay."

He headed for the den and said, "Check the bedrooms upstairs. See if there's a desk or a safe."

"On my way," Nicole said.

Two minutes later Wilde heard, "Hey, come on up here."

"You got something?"

"I think so."

When he got up, Nicole pulled a painting above a dresser to the side to reveal a Molser combination safe with a face approximately 10 inches square and a circular door that consumed most of the face. Wilde had seen them before, four times right to the first number, three times left, two times right, then left to the final number.

"Can you get into it?" Nicole asked.

"Yes but not with tools," he said.

On a shelf inside the closet, they found ten shoeboxes stuffed with photo-club porn. Wilde shuffled through each of them just enough to determine that there was nothing hidden underneath.

There wasn't.

There were only photos.

They found nothing of interest anywhere else in the house and headed for the MG. "It feels like a glacier storm out here," Wilde said. "I thought I was going to pass out in there. I really did."

Nicole locked her arm through his.

"We need to toughen you up," she said.

"People have tried," he said. "It doesn't work."

53

Day Two
July 16
Wednesday Afternoon

Danton searched every inch of Spencer's house, expecting Kent Dawson to jump out with a knife at every turn, but in the end found the place empty. "His car's still in the driveway. He must have run. I don't get it."

"He's picking his time," Ying said.

"Why? What's wrong with now?"

"He wants to find what he's looking for first," she said. "Once he has his hooks back in me, he'll try to make me get you out of town. He'll use me for leverage. That way he won't have to confront you head-on."

"He already did, though," Danton said.

"Maybe he's thinking twice about killing you."

"Why?"

She shrugged.

"I don't think it's because he's afraid of a confrontation," she said. "I think it's more because he's realized it's a pretty serious offense. If he got caught he'd lose his freedom. He knows I'd turn him in, too, even with his hooks in me."

Danton sat down on the couch.

"So what was he looking for exactly?"

Ying looked away.

"I don't want to get into it," she said.

"Why not?"

"Because I don't want you to think about me in the way that you will." She wrapped her arms around him and pressed her body tight. "There probably won't be a better time to say it than now so I'm just going to do it. You and me have something."

Danton nodded.

That was true.

"I want the past to disappear," she said. "All I want is a future and I want it to be with you."

He kissed her.

"Done." A beat then, "Now what?"

"Let me look around," she said. "I know what I'm looking for. Just stand guard in case he comes back."

Suddenly a car engine fired. Danton pulled the curtain aside to see Dawson squealing down the driveway in reverse. In the street, he slammed into the door of a parked Ford 3100 pickup before getting the vehicle fishtailing down the street.

"I've seen better drivers," Danton said.

Ying smiled.

Danton looked into her eyes and said, "My past isn't exactly pristine. I've done some things I'm not proud of. If you really do want a future together you're going to need to know what I've done and vice versa. Trust me, there's nothing you could possibly tell me that would have an impact."

She stared out the window.

"In that case just let me leave it unsaid, at least for now," she said. "Let me get searching. I'm wasting time."

"It will go faster if I help."

Ying bit her lower lip.

"I'll do it," she said.

Danton frowned.

"I'm disappointed. You don't trust me." A pause then, "It's okay, I understand. Trust is something you have to earn. The last thing you need is a third person to get their hooks in you."

Ying exhaled.

"Whether I find what I'm looking for or not, I need Dawson dead. Will you do that for me?"

54

Day Two
July 16
Wednesday Afternoon

Back at the office Yardley found twenty-seven Dawsons in the phone book. It would take a lot of snooping and running around to figure out which was the right one, not to mention that none of them might be.

Even if she found him, what would she do?

One option would be to call him anonymously and say, *I'm the woman from the house. I'm no threat to you. I'll never tell anyone so just forget I even exist.*

Would that work?

Probably not.

In fact, definitely not.

She'd still be a threat.

She couldn't un-become a threat simply by talking.

Plus, the call would be an announcement that she not only saw him at the house but also tracked him down.

Not good.

Maybe she should call the police and make an anonymous report that Spencer's body was out by the railroad tracks and that a man named Dawson killed him. Picturing herself doing that made her palms sweat.

No.

No.

No.

That would get her involved throat-deep.

She didn't have the time or energy for it.

She needed to concentrate on the scroll.

Suddenly a knock came at the door.

The client?

Here to interrogate her?

Standing there was the last person on earth she expected, namely Stephen Zipp, an associate attorney who had the office two doors down from hers back when she was employed with Bender, Littlepage & Price, P.C.

He was average height.

Average build.

Average looks.

Average everything.

He wore black glasses, just like Yardley. That was the one thing she'd always liked about him, that and the fact that he got a little weak-kneed whenever he was around her. She hadn't seen him, or even thought of him for that matter, for over a year.

He was as surprised as she was.

"Oh, you're here," he said.

"Yes."

"I didn't expect you."

"Did you come by before?"

He nodded.

"A couple of times," he said. "I'm not good at this kind of

thing so I'm just going to come out and say it. I was hoping that maybe we could have dinner sometime or go to a movie or something like that. You know, catch up on old times."

She hesitated.

Then said, "Look, Stephen, that sounds great but your timing's bad. I have more things going on right now than the law allows. I don't even have time to breathe."

He diverted his eyes.

"Okay. I understand."

"It's not you, it's just that the timing's bad. Honest, maybe in a month or two, after I get things settled."

He turned.

"Sure, I'll call you then."

Then he left.

Yardley closed the door, took a number of deep breaths and almost went after him. As she reached for the knob, though, a chill went up her spine.

Stephen was with her old law firm.

So was Taylor Lee.

Did Taylor send him here to be a spy?

If so, would it be better to shut him out or get closer to him?

Think.

Think.

Think.

Suddenly she pulled the door open and bounded down the stairs two at a time, still not sure if she was going to talk to him or just watch him leave.

55

Day Two
July 16
Wednesday Afternoon

In the back office Wilde pointed three fans at the middle of the back room, turned the lights off, pinned Nicole on the floor and kissed her.

"You're so evil," she said.

"You have no idea." He unbuttoned her blouse and ran his tongue up her stomach. "This doesn't replace what's going to happen tonight. It's in addition."

He took her slowly.

Erotically.

Bringing her to a slow boil.

Memorizing every movement of her body.

Afterwards when he opened the door and stepped into the main room, something happened that he didn't expect, namely Alabama was sitting behind the desk with her feet propped up.

"How long have you been here?" he asked.

"Long enough."

Wilde lit two cigarettes, handed one to Nicole then turned

to Alabama as he blew smoke. "Forget everything you heard," he said. "It will make you go blind."

She smiled.

"Especially the French part," he added. Then to Nicole, "What were you saying anyway?"

She laughed.

"Beige," she said. "We should paint the ceiling beige."

"Good one." To Alabama, "So what'd you get today? Anything?"

"I didn't get as much as you, but I got a few things."

Alabama's story was one Wilde didn't see coming. Warner Raven, using the name Mark Pinkard, frequented the Morning Glory brothel up on Colfax quite a bit. He had a particular fondness for a 21-year-old beauty named Wildflower, who let him get kinky.

"Kinky how?"

"He'd tie her up."

"And do what?"

She shrugged.

"I don't know, I didn't get into it," she said. "But here's the interesting part. Wildflower dropped off the face of the earth two months ago." Wilde cocked his head. "At the same time, Raven stopped going to the brothel."

"Interesting."

"I thought you'd say that," she said. "There's more. Now he's going to another brothel, one called Pirate's Cove."

Wilde knew the place.

It was over on Market.

He could walk there in six minutes.

"Is he getting kinky there?"

"They wouldn't say," Alabama said. "All I could find out is

that he uses only one of the women there, someone named Anne Bonny."

"Anne Bonny is the name of a female pirate," Wilde said. "If memory serves me, she was Calico Michael's woman."

Nicole looked puzzled.

"How would you possibly know that?"

"It's called the GI bill," he said. "To get your degree they make you learn all kinds of things you don't want to learn."

"You went to college?"

He nodded.

"Guilty."

"Under the GI bill—"

"Right."

"So you were in the war?"

True.

He was.

"Air force. I was a gunner in a B-52," he said. "I was the guy who sits in the bubble under the plane and pulls the trigger if the bad guys show up."

"I didn't know that," she said.

"Well, now you do."

"Did you ever shoot anyone down?"

"Had to," he said. "That was my job." A pause then, "Want to see my war scar?"

She did.

She did indeed.

Wilde pulled his hair up to show his left ear. On close examination, there was a slight dip at the top. "A bullet took that off. One inch over and you'd be talking to a bag of bones right now."

Wilde filled Alabama in on the fact that he and Nicole had

made an unexpected visit to Raven's house. He told her about the wall safe and the ten boxes of photo-club porn.

"I'll go over there later and go through the photos for you," Alabama said.

Wilde shook his head.

"I already checked," he said. "There's nothing in the boxes except photos."

"Did you look at every one to see if the woman was Jessica Dent or Constance Black?" she asked. "Because if they are, you have your connection."

Wilde looked at Nicole.

"Why didn't I think of that?" he asked.

"Good question."

56

Day Two
July 16
Wednesday Evening

The plan was simple. Danton and Ying took positions across the street from the hotel and waited for the hitwoman, Nicole Wickliff, to show up. Now, early evening, the sun was softer, the shadows were longer and the air had lost its bite.

The asphalt was no longer sticky.

In another hour, it would be downright nice.

Danton wouldn't admit it but he was nervous about tonight.

Dawson would come for him.

One of them would die.

A cab pulled to the curb and a sensuous woman stepped out.

"That's her," Ying said.

Danton nodded.

"Stay here."

He headed across the street at a brisk walk, followed the woman across the lobby and entered the elevator with her. She looked at him and said, "What floor?" The words were in English but had a French accent.

"Trois," Danton said.

The woman didn't move and instead wrinkled her face, surprised to hear a French word. Danton reached past her and pressed three. Heartbeats later the space shuttered and started to climb.

"You're in town to kill Emmanuelle Martin," Danton said.

The woman stared at him.

Then she tilted her head inquisitively and said, "And how is it exactly that you know that? Did Petracca send you here to help me?"

"No," Danton said. "I'm going to say something and only say it once so listen very carefully. There's a train leaving Denver at nine o'clock tonight. Be on it. If you're not, then I'm not going to have any choice but to do something I'd rather not do."

"Like what? Kill me?"

The elevator jolted to a stop.

A bell rang.

Danton stepped out and said, "Nine o'clock."

The woman laughed.

"Don't run off," she said. "We're just getting to know each other. Why don't you come to my room for a drink? We'll have a party."

"Nine o'clock," Danton said.

The woman hardened her face.

Sternly.

Defiantly.

"That's not going to happen."

Danton headed off.

He didn't turn around.

He kept his face pointed straight ahead and said, "Nine o'clock."

57

Day Two
July 16
Wednesday Evening

There weren't that many female attorneys in Denver and when men stumbled on them their natural tendency was to get them on their backs and put a new notch in their belt. Yardley didn't know why that was but did know that it was what it was. Case in point, lots of men even tried to get her in bed, as plain as she was. So she needed to be careful of Stephen for that reason alone, not to mention that he might be a spy for Taylor Lee.

They met at Keables Sandwich Shop at 18th and Stout early evening, took seats at the end of the counter and ordered burgers and cokes.

She wore a grey skirt and a white blouse.

Stephen still wore his suit but had the tie loose.

The talk was small.

Yardley purposely kept it off the law firm and off Taylor Lee.

Suddenly, the small got big when Stephen said, "Hey, you're still in good with Taylor Lee, aren't you?"

Right.

She was.

They met for coffee or lunch every couple of weeks.

"So what was it that almost got her canned back in February?"

"What are you talking about?"

"I won't tell anyone," he said. "I was just curious."

"I don't know anything about it."

"She never mentioned it?"

No.

She didn't.

"So she almost got canned?"

Stephen nodded.

"Don't say you heard it from me, but there were pretty strong rumors going around the halls that she had screwed something up," he said. "We all expected her to mysteriously be gone one day, with some kind of announcement that she'd quit to take a job somewhere else or some such thing. Then all of a sudden everything seemed back to normal. I never could figure it out."

"If something was going on, she never told me."

"Okay."

"Honest," Yardley said.

"I believe you."

Yardley sucked coke out of a bottle through a straw and asked, "Do you work with her on any cases?"

No.

Never.

"She'll say hello in the hall if we pass but that's about it," he said.

"She's pretty, don't you think?"

Yes.

He did.

"Stunning," he said. "Did I say that out loud?"

Yardley smiled and nodded.

"Don't repeat it, okay?"

She pulled an imaginary zipper across her lips.

Then she said something she didn't expect. "After we eat, do you want to take a walk or something?"

Stephen looked at his watch.

"Sure, but it'll have to be quick. I have a photo-club meeting at eight."

Yardley wrinkled her face.

"You're in one of those?"

"Yeah, why?"

"I don't know. I just never pictured you as the type."

58

Day Two
July 16
Wednesday Evening

While Nicole took a cab to her hotel to shower off the heat and change into fresh clothes, Wilde bought Alabama a sandwich and salad at Baur's on Curtis Street.

"So what's the plan for tonight?" she asked.

Wilde chewed what was in his mouth and said, "I've been contemplating on whether to let you go through Raven's camera-club photos. The more I think about it the more I don't like it."

"Why not?"

"Play it through," he said. "Suppose he actually is the killer. And suppose, just for the sake of argument, he catches you in his house. What do you think will happen next?"

Alabama brushed it off.

"He won't catch me. There's no way."

Wilde shook his head.

"It's a bad idea," he said. "I can't let you take the risk."

She slapped him on the face, softly, but enough to get his

attention.

"Read my lips," she said. "This needs to be done. It's going to take hours. Who else is going to do it if I don't?"

"I'll do it."

"Look," she said. "The boxes are in his bedroom closet and the bedroom has a window, right?"

Wilde nodded.

"Correct."

"Wilde," she said, "if I say right, and it is right, you're supposed to say right, not correct."

He smiled.

"Sorry."

"When you say correct you're just upsetting the balance of the universe."

"My fault."

"What I'll do is leave the bedroom window open while I'm in there," she said. "If he happens to come home, I'll just jump out. I'm a good jumper. I know how to roll."

Wilde thought it through.

He still didn't like it.

Alabama squeezed his hand.

"You're getting me off the streets," she said "You're even letting me move in with you."

Wilde winced.

He'd forgotten about that.

Well, that wasn't exactly true.

He hadn't forgotten, he just hadn't had time to think about it much.

"By the way, they delivered the futon this afternoon," Alabama said. "The bottom line is you need to let me earn my keep. I don't want any handouts."

Wilde shook his head.

"I'll tell you what, you can pay for the dinner."

"Bryson, you know what I mean," she said. "I know it's risky. I appreciate that. I'll be careful, I promise. I can also get into the safe while I'm there."

The words took Wilde by surprise.

"You know how to break into a safe?"

She rolled her eyes at the absurdity of the question.

"We'll hang around outside his house tonight," she said. "If he goes out, you and Nicole follow him and I'll head in." She held her hand out to shake. "Deal?"

Wilde hesitated.

Then he shook her hand and said, "Deal, but just for the record, I'm still the boss."

Alabama laughed.

"You stopped being the boss the minute you hired me," she said.

"Yeah, well, you know it and I know it but the rest of the world doesn't so at least pretend, especially when Nicole's around."

Alabama studied him.

"Don't fall for her, Bryson."

"Why not?"

"I don't know. Just don't."

He smiled.

"You know what bad advice is?"

No.

She didn't.

"When you have good advice but deliver it too late, that's bad advice."

59

Day Two
July 16
Wednesday Night

Wednesday night after dark Danton and Ying were stopped at a red light at Broadway and Colfax when a taxi skirted through the intersection. Danton's heart raced.

"Follow that taxi," he said.

"Why?"

"Emmanuelle's in it."

"Are you sure?"

"Pretty sure."

Ying waited for green then made a quick left on Colfax and stepped on the gas. Two blocks later the taxi pulled to the curb and stopped. Ying did the same, staying as far back as she could.

A woman got out of the taxi and headed east on foot.

Danton and Ying got out and followed.

"Is that Emmanuelle's walk?"

Yes.

It was.

"I'm almost positive," Danton said.

The woman zigzagged through the streets, farther and farther into the mansions of Capitol Hill.

She never turned around.

"What the hell is she doing?" Ying asked.

"I don't know."

Suddenly the woman disappeared into the yard of a stately mansion. Danton and Ying kept walking at a normal pace, to all intents and purposes just two people from the neighborhood out for a stroll. When they got to where the woman dropped off, they looked in that direction.

A flashlight flickered inside a dark house.

Just for an instance, then it was gone.

"I know that house," Ying said.

"You do?"

"It belongs to a socialite named Grace Somerfield. She was murdered in there Saturday night."

"Really?"

Yes.

Really.

"Someone robbed her and slit her throat," she said. "So what's your friend Emmanuelle doing in there?"

"Good question."

60

Day Two
July 16
Wednesday Night

Yardley got home Wednesday evening to find a man sitting on the sofa in the dark smoking a cigarette. He didn't make a move when the lights went on. He just sat there staring at her. She had time to run back out the door but didn't. She knew who the man was—he was big, with long hair and a hard, manly face. Strong arms stuck out of a T-shirt. The sleeves were rolled up, the left one held a pack of cigarettes. In other circumstances he would have been attractive.

"You're Taylor Lee's client," she said.

The man flicked ashes onto the floor.

"Very good," he said. "I want the scroll and I want it now."

"Someone stole it."

He wrinkled his face.

"Is that so?"

Yes.

It was.

"Who would do such a thing? No one knew you had it besides Taylor Lee."

"A professor knew I had it," Yardley said. "I took it to her to learn about it."

"Are you saying she stole it?"

"I don't know who stole it," Yardley said. "Maybe she told someone about it. Maybe that person told someone else. All I know is that someone broke in here when I wasn't home and took it."

The man stood up, walked to the window and looked down.

Then he turned and said, "It's not yours."

"I know that."

"I don't think you understand what's going on here," he said.

"Look, I'm sorry that—"

The man took a step towards her and pointed an index finger at her chest.

"Don't," he said. "Here's what you're going to do. You're going to get that scroll back into the hands of Taylor Lee by noon tomorrow."

"But—"

"Stop! Don't say a word. Just listen. You're going to get that scroll back into the hands of Taylor Lee by noon tomorrow. She's going to give it to me. I'm going to go away. We're all going to live happily ever after."

Yardley swallowed.

"That's impossible."

"We both know you're lying," he said. "If noon comes tomorrow and I don't get a call from Taylor Lee to come by her office and pick it up, two things are going to happen. Do you want to know what they are?"

Yardley shook her head.

"No."

"Too bad because I'm going to tell you anyway," the man said. "First, Taylor Lee is going to die. It won't be pretty. It won't be pretty at all. Second, you'll be next. Am I being clear enough?"

He flicked his cigarette at her.

It bounced off her forehead and fell to the floor.

The man walked over, ground it out with his foot and gave Yardley a kiss on the cheek.

"Noon tomorrow."

Then he was gone.

61

Day Two
July 16
Wednesday Night

Wednesday night the brutal heat of the day dissipated into the thin Rocky Mountain air and life got bearable again. Wilde and Alabama sat in the MG a half-block down from Warner Raven's house, waiting for him to head out into the darkness and steal a woman. Wilde had a Camel cupped in his hand with the tip out of sight.

Nicole was supposed to call him early in the evening, when she was ready to be picked up.

She never called.

Wilde swung by her hotel an hour ago.

She wasn't in her room.

She hadn't checked out.

No one at the front desk had seen her all day.

"What are you going to do if you catch him in the act?" Alabama asked.

"You mean, actually taking someone?"

Right.

That.

"I don't know, I haven't thought about it."

Alabama sighed.

"How did you manage to stay alive before I came along?"

Wilde dipped his hat lower.

"It's a mystery, isn't it?" A pause then, "I wonder where Nicole is."

"I don't know."

Wilde took one last drag on the cigarette and flicked it into the street.

"The main thing tonight is for you to stay safe," he said. "Keep that window open. If there's any chance at all that he's back, get out of there. Do you have the suitcase picture of Constance Black and Jessica Dent?"

Alabama felt inside her pants pocket to be sure.

"Yes."

"Check the flashlight to be sure it works."

She flicked it on.

"All right," Wilde said. "If one of the camera-club pictures turns out to be Constance or Jessica, take it with you but try to remember which box it came out of."

"Got it."

"I shouldn't be letting you do this," he said. "I'm going to go to hell."

Alabama smiled.

"Wrong about the first part, right about the second."

"Thanks for the encouragement."

"No problem."

Ten minutes later, Raven bounded out of the house and flicked a cigarette towards the street as he slipped into 1948 Nash Air-flyte.

"We're up," Wilde said.

Alabama got out and slipped into the shadows.

"Good luck."

"You too."

Wilde waited until Raven got to the end of the street, then followed.

Nicole.

Nicole.

Nicole.

Where are you?

What's going on?

62

Day Two
July 16
Wednesday Night

Danton and Ying hung in the shadows across the street from Grace Somerfield's house waiting for Emmanuelle to come out. Ten minutes into it, they caught a flashlight splashing across an upstairs wall, there for a microsecond and then gone just as fast. After that they got nothing. An hour passed. Danton's pacing got more and more pronounced.

"She left out the other side," he said.

"We don't know that."

"It's been too quiet for too long," he said. "Wait here. I'm going to go in."

"What for?"

Suddenly the silhouette of a person appeared in the back yard, barely perceptible against an almost-equal darkness. Danton nudged Ying and said, "Shhh." The figure made it to the sidewalk and then headed away at a brisk pace.

They followed.

The woman came under a streetlight.

It was definitely Emmanuelle.

She wasn't holding anything.

Her arms swung freely.

"If she was looking for anything bigger than a piece of paper, she didn't find it," Danton said.

The plan was simple.

Follow her.

Find out where she was staying.

Then regroup.

Emmanuelle took a right at the first side street, temporarily masked by a string of hedges. When Danton and Ying got to the same corner and looked down the street, Emmanuelle wasn't where she should be.

She wasn't anywhere.

Danton made a fist and pounded it into his other hand.

"She spotted us," he said. "She's gone."

Silence.

Then Ying said, "Now what?"

Danton turned and headed back towards the car. "Now we need to get into that house and figure out what she was search-ing for," he said.

"Now?"

"Yes," he said. "We'll need flashlights though."

"I have one in the trunk."

"You're such a prepared little criminal."

"I don't know if the batteries are any good."

The batteries weren't perfect but they were strong enough. The back door lock had been pried out with a screwdriver, a clumsy job that looked like what a teen might do. They entered and found themselves in a kitchen.

Emmanuelle, it turned out, hadn't been neat.

Drawers were pulled out and left that way.

Cabinet doors hung open.

Cushions were tossed.

Books were scooped off shelves.

Upstairs in the master bedroom was a wall safe, unlocked with the door hanging open.

Nothing was inside.

The master closet had been ransacked.

"What are we looking for exactly?" Ying asked.

"We'll know it when we see it," Danton said. "Whatever it is, it's still here somewhere. I can smell it."

63

Day Two
July 16
Wednesday Night

After the man left, Yardley grabbed her one and only bottle of wine, unscrewed the top and took a long drink. The alcohol stung her mouth but felt good when it dropped into her stomach.

Everything softened.

She took another swig, looked out the window for a few moments and then sat down on the couch.

Noon tomorrow.

That's how long she had.

Now what?

64

Day Two
July 16
Wednesday Night

As Wilde tailed Raven through the Denver nightscape, the interior of the MG was cold and empty and his blood was slow. Nicole should be sitting right there, right next to him, right now. She wasn't. What the hell was going on?

Where was she?

If she changed her mind about him, why?

What did he do?

How did he suddenly fall short?

Raven pulled Wilde down 8th Avenue into downtown, then west into that jagged industrial area by the South Platte. The traffic thinned, the asphalt turned to gravel, then the gravel turned to dirt. Wilde had to drop back, even out of sight at times, and finally turned his headlights off altogether. Broken warehouses of abandoned war-related industries cluttered the area.

He came to an intersection.

The taillights of a car were stopped a block down. They

brightened for a heartbeat then went out altogether.

Wilde backed up out of sight and killed the engine.

Then he hugged the shadows and headed down the street on foot.

This would be a perfect place to stash a woman for a day or two.

Is that what Raven was doing?

Was he stopping by to check up on someone?

Wilde took one quiet, purposeful step at a time.

He should have brought the gun.

He spotted a rusty piece of rebar in the dirt and picked it up.

It was nasty in his hand.

He didn't care.

In thirty seconds it might save his life.

65

Day Two
July 16
Wednesday Night

After an unsuccessful hour inside Grace Somerfield's house, Danton and Ying headed home to find Kent Dawson's car in the driveway. Ying stopped in the street, shifted into neutral and stared at it in disbelief.

"What do we do?"

Danton studied the vehicle.

Silently.

The confrontation was here.

Someone was going to be dead very soon.

It might be him.

"Wait here," he said. "Keep the engine running. If Dawson comes your way, get the hell out of here and don't come back."

"Degare!"

He stopped at her side of the car, leaned in and kissed her. Then he headed for the house.

Dawson was sitting on the sofa smoking a cigarette.

"I told you to be out of town by dark," he said.

"It looks like I didn't listen," Danton said.

Dawson smiled.

"No, it looks like you didn't. So now we need to wrap things up. I've been sitting here, thinking about how best to do it. I've come up with an idea. You want to hear it?"

Danton leaned against the wall and crossed his arms.

"Go ahead."

"I propose that you and me get in my car and drive somewhere where no one's going to bother us," he said. "Then we settle it, man to man, with just our fists. A fight to the death."

"Where were you thinking of doing it?"

Dawson shrugged.

"My guess is that after you killed Spencer, you dumped him somewhere off the beaten path. Why don't we do it there? It'd be sort of fitting, don't you think?"

Danton considered it.

"Wait here," he said.

He walked out to Ying, leaned in the window and said, "Me and Dawson are going to take a little ride. I'll be back in an hour, an hour-fifteen tops. I'm going to need you to stitch me up when I get back. If you don't have the supplies, go out and get them while I'm gone."

"Degare!"

He kissed her.

"It's going to be fine," he said. "Pick up some whiskey too."

He walked back into the house and said, "Let's go."

66

Day Two
July 16
Wednesday Night

With a half bottle of wine in her gut, Yardley locked her apartment, got on her Schwinn Spitfire bicycle and pointed the front tire south on Santa Fe. A half hour later she pounded on the front door of a dark house. No one came. She kept pounding until a very surprised Taylor Lee pulled it open.

"We need to talk," Yardley said.

"Have you been drinking?"

Yardley pushed past her.

"I need to use your bathroom first."

Then, after first things first, she told Taylor about the client's visit, particularly the fact that if he didn't have the scroll in hand by noon tomorrow, he'd kill Taylor first then Yardley.

Taylor's hands shook.

"Was he serious or was he just shaking the tree?"

"Serious."

"Are you sure?"

Yardley nodded.

"Positive."

"So what do we do, call the police or hire a bodyguard?"

Yardley frowned.

"I saw you in the cab last night," she said.

Taylor tilted her head.

Confused.

"What?"

"You know what I'm talking about," Yardley said. "I already told you about that man who came over to my house last night pretending to be my client and demanding the scroll. I had it right there in my apartment and could have given it to him, but he was clearly a fake. He wasn't a real client, he was a puppet with someone else pulling the strings."

"Right, you told me that."

"What I didn't tell you is that when he left, I followed him to a payphone," Yardley said. "He made a call and then got picked up by a cab. In the backseat of that cab was a woman. *That woman was you.*"

Taylor shook her head.

"That's crazy."

"I saw you."

"There's no way you could have seen me because whoever you saw wasn't me," Taylor said.

"Just admit it was you and tell me why you did it," Yardley said.

Taylor stood up and opened the front door.

"It's time for you to leave."

Yardley walked out.

The ride home was long and lonely.

She hadn't gotten what she went for. She was hoping to

read something in Taylor's face or hear something in her voice to find out if she was the woman in the cab.

She didn't get that.

She still wasn't sure.

67

Day Two
July 16
Wednesday Night

The remoteness of the area and the darkness of the night sharpened Wilde's animal instincts. He wasn't walking, he was hunting. He wasn't breathing, he was feeding his lungs. He wasn't seeing, he was absorbing.

A bad, bad thought entered his brain.

Raven abducted Nicole this afternoon.

That's why she never called.

She would be Friday's kill.

Maybe Raven got a whiff that Alabama had been running down his dark side. Maybe he traced Alabama to Wilde. Maybe taking Nicole was his cute little idea of revenge.

Wilde tightened his grip on the rebar. The rust poisoned his pores and grated his skin. His human instinct was to throw it down and wash his hands. His animal instinct was to embrace it. Raven was a strong man and an ex-Marine. Wilde wasn't sure he could take him in a fair fight.

The Nash Airflyte got closer and closer.

Wilde approached as invisibly as he could.

Raven wasn't in the vehicle.

The closest structure was a large, steel pre-fabricated shell with no windows, a man-door and a row of overhead doors on a truck dock. The man-door was locked. None of the dock doors would push up. There was a door on the side and two more on the back. All of them were locked. No sounds came from within.

Strange.

Wouldn't Raven park in front of the building he'd enter?

Maybe not.

Maybe he didn't want the car to be a calling card.

Wilde walked to the next building, an abandoned cinder-block structure with sporadic pane windows, most of which were busted out. He stuck his head in, careful to keep his face away from the jags. No sounds, lights or vibrations came from inside. If Nicole was in there, Wilde would be able to feel her.

He moved on.

The third building was more of the same.

So was the next.

And the next.

Then Wilde spotted something.

It was a large, menacing silhouette, blacker than the night around it.

It had an evil edge to it.

Wilde headed towards it with a nervous walk.

Nicole was in there.

He could feel her.

He'd never killed anyone with his bare hands.

Raven would be the first.

Wilde wouldn't worry about it afterwards.

He'd never second-guess what he was about to do.

Four stories, maybe five, that's how tall the structure was as Wilde got closer to it. The front door was locked but a broken side window was low enough to climb through. Inside, the structure was so absolutely pitch-black that it may as well have been at the bottom of the world's deepest cave.

He held his breath perfectly quiet and listened.

He heard nothing.

He listened harder.

Still nothing.

That didn't mean no one was there. Raven could be on another floor, or in a room behind a closed door, plus he might not be making any noise. Nicole might be unconscious. Raven might be cupped against her, silently licking her face or twisting her nipples or sliding his dick in and out of her thighs.

Wilde stuck his arms out, mummy-like, and took one careful step after another, deeper and deeper into the guts of the hellhole.

Suddenly he remembered the matches and checked his pocket.

He had six packs.

If he lit one, it would give him away.

He didn't care and lit up.

It provided a lot less light than he anticipated, hardly any actually, given the depth of the space. It was enough to let him see something of interest.

The floor was concrete, something he had already figured out.

Two steps in front of him was a large brownish stain.

Blood?

He walked over, squatted down and took a closer look.

A rat ran down the edge of the floor, drawing Wilde's attention for a second.

The fire inched its way to his flesh.

He tossed it down and lit a fresh one.

Blood.

That's what the stain was.

Blood.

He'd seen enough in his life to know.

68

Day Two
July 16
Wednesday Night

D anton stared straight out the windshield as Dawson drove through the Denver nightscape. Neither man talked. In thirty minutes they turned right down a service road next to railroad tracks. A few miles later Danton said, "Stop."

Dawson pulled over but left the engine running and the headlights on.

Both men stepped out.

A rancid odor came from a rotting body next to a rabbit brush.

Dawson made a face and said, "Is that Spencer?"

"It is," Danton said. "Take a good look because it's going to be you too."

Both men walked to the front of the vehicle where they could see each other in the headlights.

Suddenly a large knife flashed in Dawson's hand.

"I thought you said bare hands," Danton said.

"It looks like I lied."

The man charged.

Danton reacted too slowly.

The knife caught him on the ear.

Blood immediately ran down his neck. He put his hand on it to get a feel for the quantity and pulled it back sopping wet. He needed to get this done, right now, before the loss of blood got him weak.

He let out a war cry at the top of his lungs and charged.

Dawson would have been harder to kill than Spencer, except for the fact that Dawson brought a knife to the fight, a knife that got wrestled out of his grip and then got stabbed in his left eye all the way down to the handle.

After the man stopped twitching, Danton pulled the weapon out and wiped it clean on Dawson's pants.

A souvenir.

He dragged Dawson's body over to Spencer's rotting corpse and threw it on top.

There.

Done.

Rot in hell.

Both of you.

Dawson wanted a fight to the death.

Now he'd been obliged.

Danton turned the car around and took one last look at the bodies.

"Be careful what you ask for," he said.

Then he got the hell out of there.

Ying was free.

Danton couldn't wait to tell her.

Free.

Free.

Free.

DAY THREE

July 17
Thursday

69

Day Three
July 17
Thursday Morning

A pounding at the door pulled Yardley out of a wine-induced, cavern-deep unconsciousness Thursday morning. She opened her eyes just enough to see daylight squirting around the window coverings. Judging by the strength, she'd slept into mid-morning.

Pound.

Pound.

Pound.

"Hold on."

She ruffled her hair, grabbed her glasses and staggered for the door. Standing there was the last person she expected to see.

Taylor Lee.

The woman handed her a large cup of coffee in a disposable cup. "Peace offering," she said.

Yardley took a careful sip.

It was hot.

Just what she needed.

"Sorry about last night," she said. "I was mostly drunk. I don't know if that was you or not in the cab. I was trying to shake your tree and see if you'd admit it."

"It wasn't me," Taylor said.

"Okay."

"Honest."

"I believe you."

"What we need to do is figure out who it was," Taylor said. "They're the ones who stole the scroll. Like I said before, it could be my fault because I told someone what was going on, namely Mark Creighton."

Yardley remembered the conversation.

She also remembered the man.

Creighton was one of the upper-echelon partners in Bender, Littlepage & Pierce. Yardley never liked him, not because he was a womanizer, although that was part of it, but because he was also a silent partner in an organization that operated a number of whore houses, both here in Denver and up in Central City.

"I talked to Creighton this morning," Taylor said. "He swore up and down that he never told anyone about the scroll. He never repeated our conversation to anyone." A pause then, "I believe him. He's partially scum, we both know that, but he's not a very good liar. If he'd been lying, I would have picked up on it."

Yardley made a face.

She had to use the facilities.

Not in three seconds, now.

"I'm going to shower," she said. "Make yourself at home."

Twenty minutes later she emerged from the bathroom with damp skin wrapped in a white bathrobe, toweling her hair, to find Taylor in the kitchen with her jacket off and sleeves rolled up, flipping pancakes in a frying pan.

"Another peace offering," she said.

Yardley sat at the table.

"When you make peace, you don't mess around."

Taylor smiled.

"No, I don't."

Yardley fumbled through the cabinets until she found the syrup, then said, "If it's true that the leak didn't come from your end then it came from mine. The only person I told about the scroll and in particular the fact that it mysteriously arrived from a purported client was the university professor, Blanche Twister."

Right.

Taylor knew that.

"We need to focus on her, right now, this morning," Taylor said.

Yardley considered it.

She knew that Twister wasn't behind any theft, because there had been no real theft. Still, it would be valuable to know if she was the woman in the cab because if she was then Taylor wasn't. That meant Taylor was clean. Knowing whether Taylor was trustworthy or not was worth knowing.

She looked at Taylor and said, "Let's do it. But how?"

"Just use the same trick you tried with me," Taylor said. "Tell her you saw her in the cab and see if she admits it."

"Okay."

"Get dressed, we're wasting time."

70

Day Three
July 17
Thursday Morning

Coffee, the sweet aroma of coffee, that's what Wilde woke to Thursday morning, that and the rustling of movement in the kitchen. At first it confused him, then he remembered that Alabama had moved in. He took a shower, wrapped a towel around his waist and headed for the kitchen as he combed wet hair back.

Alabama grinned at the sight.

"I have half a mind to yank that towel down," she said.

Wilde scowled.

"Don't even think about it."

"Okay," she said.

When Wilde stepped over, she yanked it down with a cat-quick move he never saw coming.

His jaw dropped.

He grabbed the towel from her hand and re-wrapped it.

Alabama laughed and said, "Lighten up, we're going to see each other naked now and then, living together. Now we have it over with, at least as far as your part of it goes." Then she pulled her shorts down and her blouse up, wiggled her body and then turned around in a few circles before putting every-thing back in place. "Those are the panties you bought me. There, we're even. Don't you feel better?"

He paused.

Then laughed.

"Well, I guess we got it over with."

"Yes we did."

She poured him coffee, scooped four piping hot waffles onto a plate and set them on the table next to butter and straw-berry jam.

Wilde sat down and dug in.

"Delicious."

"The food or me?"

He smiled.

"Both."

"Right answer," she said. "You're learning."

As the food began to jump-start his brain, he thought about last night, which had been both good and bad. On the bad side, he spent a full hour walking in the dark through the eerie building trying to find Nicole and/or Raven.

He found nothing.

When he checked to make sure Raven's car was still around, it wasn't. He got worried that Raven would go home and catch Alabama in his bedroom, so he abandoned his search for Ni-cole and headed that way.

That was the bad part of it.

The good part of it was that Alabama did as she was sup-posed to, namely keep the window open and drop down if she heard anything. It turned out that the window had already been left half open by Raven, so it wouldn't arouse suspicion when he got home and found it that way.

That was the good part of it.

Even better though was that just before Raven came home, Alabama came across what she was looking for, namely camera-club photos of Jessica Dent. "There were thirty or forty pictures of her," she said. "I just took these five."

When Wilde looked at them, there was no question.

The woman in the photos was Jessica Dent.

"So he knew her," Wilde said.

"Yes he did."

"We have our connection."

"Yes we do."

"All the time he sat in my office handing me the case, he led on like he'd never heard of or seen Jessica Dent at any time in his life," Wilde said. "That speaks volumes, doesn't it?"

Alabama nodded.

Yes.

It did.

At that point in the night, Wilde's brain and body gave out. He had to get home and get some sleep.

Now it was morning, a morning filled with coffee and waffles.

Wilde picked up the plate and continued eating as he headed for the bathroom.

"Where you going?" Alabama asked.

"Getting dressed."

"What's the rush?"

"The rush is Nicole."

"What does that mean, that you're heading back to that warehouse area to look for her?"

"That's exactly what it means."

"I'm going with you," she said.

Silence.

"I said I'm going with you," Alabama repeated.

"I heard you."

"And?"

"And what?"

"And, where's the argument?" Alabama asked.

"There isn't one."

"Does that mean I can go?"

"It looks that way."

"Good," she said. "We're going to need flashlights. Do you have any?"

"Negative," he said. "We'll pick some up on the way."

A beat went by.

Then another.

And another.

"Hey, I just thought of my reward, if we find Nicole," Alabama said.

Wilde groaned.

"Don't even tell me."

"You don't want to hear it?"

"No."

"Too bad," she said, "because here it is. My reward is going to be a threesome with you and Nicole."

"Forget about it."

"Don't you think it would be fun?"

"That's not the point."

"You did it with that Asian woman," she said. "What was her name?"

"Ying."

"Right, Ying," Alabama said. "You two did it with her. I'm just as pretty, don't you think?"

Wilde headed for the closet and pulled one of his six grey suits off the hanger.

"No threesomes," he said.

"Why not?"

"Because I'm your boss," he said.

"No you're not," Alabama said. "You only think you are. We've already been over that part of it."

"Well, one of us is the boss of the other one," Wilde said. "What that means is no sex. End of discussion."

"You'll give in," Alabama said. "Get used to the idea."

"No I won't."

Three minutes later he stepped out of the bedroom, dressed except for one thing. Alabama picked that one thing off the rack—the hat—and put it on Wilde's head, perfectly tilted.

"There, complete," she said.

"Let's go."

They headed for the door.

"You know, it's the guy who is supposed to wait for the girl, not vice versa," she said.

Wilde groaned.

"This is going to be a long day."

"Actually, not," Alabama said. "The threesome will make it go by fast."

71

Day Three
July 17
Thursday Morning

Ying was still asleep when Danton woke Thursday morning. He opened his eyes briefly, then closed them and replayed the incredible passion of last night. His life had changed, how big and how far was yet to be determined, but a change had come.

Ying was someone he needed in his life.

A Denver woman.

Not a Paris woman.

That complicated things, but not to the point of failure.

He kissed her imperceptibly and headed for the shower.

Last night could have been worse.

He'd managed to wrestle the knife out of Dawson's hand early on, before his face got beaten into a Frankenstein look-alike. The ear bled profusely during the fight and for quite a while afterwards but in the end wasn't serious.

A scar, that's all he'd have.

Leaving the scene, he drove to a roadside payphone on Santa Fe and called Ying. She met him with the Packard and then followed him for thirty miles south, halfway to Colorado Springs, where they ditched Dawson's Nash on a mountain switchback.

All the time they were invisible.

No one unexpected came along when they shouldn't have.

He decided to not keep the knife for a souvenir after all and threw it in a ravine.

They drove home.

Cleaned up.

Drank whiskey.

Had drunken sex.

And passed out.

That was last night.

Now it was morning.

When Danton got out of the shower, Ying was still unconscious in bed. He left a note on the kitchen table—*Back soon*—took the Packard and headed over to Capitol Hill, parking two blocks from Grace Somerfield's house.

Then he strolled down the street towards it.

The Colorado sky was flawless.

Two magpies jumped off a Ponderosa pine and flew overhead.

His goal was to slip back into Grace's house but the nosy noses of too many nosy neighbors put the brakes on the idea. Just as Danton was strolling past, a woman came down the driveway of the house next door with a Schnauzer on a leash. Danton made a split-second decision and said, "How you doing?"

"Good."

"Did they catch anybody yet?" he asked, nodding towards the victim's house.

The woman came closer and looked around as if to be sure no one was eavesdropping.

"They have a suspect but haven't arrested her yet."

"Her?"

The woman nodded.

"Yes, a woman," she said. "I would have never thought it myself, not in a million years. Her name's Night Neveraux. That's a strange name, isn't it? Night—it even sounds like a killer's name, all dark and everything."

"Why is she a suspect?"

"The rumor is—and you didn't hear it from me—that someone saw her coming out of the back yard Saturday night and got her license plate number. The cops searched her house but didn't find any of the stolen items. That would have been enough to arrest her, in my opinion, just the fact that she was in the back yard on the night in question. But the cops seem to have a different view of it. All we can do is hope she doesn't kill anyone else while they're pussy-footing around."

"Let's hope," Danton said.

The dog tugged at the leash.

"Hold on," the woman told it. "You're French. Did you know Grace?"

"No, why? Was she French?"

"No, she's American, but she loved Paris," she said. "She's been there—oh, I don't know—six or seven times, maybe."

Danton stretched.

"It's a nice place," he said.

"So I hear."

Danton headed for the first public phone, found Night Neveraux's address in the directory, and eventually made his way to a small brick standalone house on Ogden Street between 9th and 10th. The street was lined with cars on both sides. He had to go all the way to 14th before he found an open slot, then doubled back on foot on the opposite side of the street.

The windows were up.

Fans were blowing.

Suddenly two women came out of the house.

One was a gorgeous blond.

The other was a raven-haired beauty with deep Mediterranean skin, possibly Italian or Greek.

Danton dropped down, ostensibly to tie his shoe, and disappeared behind a beat-up Chevy. When he came back up the women were sitting on the front steps sipping coffee. His instinct was to drop back down but that would be abnormal. He had no option but to walk. He kept his face straight ahead, paying them no mind, but could feel their eyes taking him in.

Just keep walking.

Keep walking.

Keep walking.

He didn't look back, not for a full block. When he finally did, he saw something he didn't expect.

The Mediterranean woman was right behind him.

Not more than a step behind.

Before he could completely turn, the woman closed the gap and pricked the point of a knife into his back.

"Do you want to die?" she asked.

"No."

72

Day Three
July 17
Thursday Morning

It took a half hour for Yardley and Taylor to get to the university, then another half hour waiting for the professor, Blanche Twister, PhD., to finish the class she was teaching. They caught her just outside the door and walked across campus with her.

"Tuesday night, someone showed up at my apartment pretending to be my client and wanting the scroll," Yardley said. "The man was a fake. Someone was pulling his strings. You're the only person in the world that knew the scroll came from a mystery client."

Twister stopped in mid-step.

"Are you implying that I initiated some kind of charade to steal the scroll from you?"

The tone was indignation.

Yardley didn't back down.

She didn't have time.

Everything was coming to a head at noon.

"I followed the so-called client when he left my apartment," she said. "He went to a public phone and made a call. Later, a cab swung by and picked him up. In the back of that cab was a woman. That woman was you."

Twister tilted her head.

"I don't know who's playing games with you, if in fact someone is," she said. "What I can absolutely assure you of is that it isn't me."

She walked away.

Yardley looked at Taylor and said, "What do you think?"

"I think she didn't look as startled as she should have."

They headed back to the car.

The sky was nice.

The air was warm.

The buzz of students brought back memories of carefree days.

The contrast was palpable.

"If she's behind the charade, we're not going to get it out of her," Yardley said. "She's too smart."

73

Day Three
July 17
Thursday Morning

A pack of stray dogs loped past as Wilde brought the roadster to a halt and killed the engine. The weed-infested dirt streets and the ragged buildings were just as abandoned as last night but not as eerie. The goal was to find Nicole even if that meant going through every single inch of every single structure.

He looked around and got his bearings.

Then he pointed and said, "You take that building, that one, that one, that one and that gray one over there."

"We're splitting up?" Alabama asked.

He nodded.

"Meet me back here in one hour even if you're not done yet," he said.

She held her wrist up.

It was barren.

"No watch," she said.

He gave her his and said, "One hour. When you look around, don't get fancy. Watch out for broken glass, especially if you have to climb through a window. Watch out for falls, don't walk on anything unstable."

She ran a finger down his chest.

"If I get a boo-boo, will you kiss it?"

Wilde ignored it.

"You know what?" he said. "On second thought, splitting up isn't a good idea. Just stick with me."

"Why?"

"Just in case Raven's around," he said. "I don't want you walking into a lair."

"You're so protective," Alabama said.

"Don't read more into it than there is," Wilde said. "All I'm trying to do is avoid having to decide whether to rescue you or not, if Raven takes you."

"You would."

"Don't be so sure."

Wilde was 99 percent sure that Nicole wasn't in any of the buildings he'd searched last night, so he started with a new one.

It was empty.

They went through a second one.

It was equally empty.

They came out the back. Wilde took his hat off and wiped sweat off his forehead. "It's going to bust a hundred again today, guaranteed."

"We'll go home later and take a cold shower together," Alabama said.

"Do you ever think of anything besides sex?"

She pondered it.

"No."

Wilde smiled.

"Where were you when I was seventeen?"

At the back of the building was a truck dock with an expansive, dirt turnaround area. A weed-infested, potholed road led from there to a shed of some sort a hundred yards away.

Wilde stared at it.

It would be a long, crumby walk.

Forget it.

He headed back towards the street then stopped and looked back at the shed.

"Let's check it out," he said.

Alabama sat down in the shade.

"I'll wait here."

Wilde looked around, saw no one and said, "I'll be right back."

He pulled out a book of matches and set it on fire as he walked.

74

Day Three
July 17
Thursday Morning

Danton could twist or make a sudden move. That would give him an edge but not a good enough one. The woman would still be able to react fast enough to stick the blade into his back.

They walked in silence.

A hundred yards, that's all he had before they'd be back at the house. Inside it would be two against one.

His veins pulsed.

Sweat rolled down his forehead.

As he reached up to wipe it off, the woman dug the point in deeper, on the verge of breaking through the skin.

"Don't," she said.

He put his hand back to his side.

Sweat dropped into his right eye.

He blinked to get it out.

Most of it squeezed out and rolled down his check. A part of it stayed in and blurred his vision.

He blinked again.

Then several times.

There.

Better.

He could see clearly again.

Fifty yards, that's all he had left now. The woman must have sensed his tension because she stuck the point in with increased purpose and said, "Don't do anything stupid."

"Who are you?"

"You know who I am," she said.

Suddenly something happened that he didn't expect.

A police car came up the street. Danton waited for the driver to look at him, then quickly waved him over.

He braced for the stab.

It didn't come.

The point came away from his back.

Danton broke away and stuck his head in the window as the car came to a stop. The woman was walking away, briskly, throwing a nervous glance over her shoulder.

"Hi," Danton said.

The cop had short hair, a thick neck and several prominent red veins on his nose.

"There was a green car racing down the street a few minutes ago at a thousand miles an hour," Danton said. "You might want to keep a lookout for him."

"What kind of car was it?"

"I don't know the make," Danton said. "It was big and green. There were two people inside."

The officer nodded.

"Thanks, I'll watch out for it."

"I just don't want to see a kid getting run over," Danton said.

"Right."

As the cop pulled away, Danton looked up the street to see the Mediterranean woman walking into Night Neveraux's house.

He headed the opposite way at a brisk pace.

75

Day Three
July 17
Thursday Morning

B ack at the law office, Yardley checked around just long enough to confirm that no one had broken in or left any dead animals inside to rattle her, then headed outside for a walk. Her whole life, she'd always done what was right, without question, without hesitation. Moral dilemmas were not things that kept her up at night.

Now, however, she had one.

She'd let herself stall this morning and no longer had the time to physically dig up the scroll and get it to Taylor by noon, even if she wanted to. That would have gotten the target off Taylor's back, Yardley's too for that matter. Life would have defaulted to a pre-scroll time, boring but safe. The dilemma was that even now she didn't want to give it up, though failing to do so might result in Taylor's murder.

She was selfish.

She hated herself.

She had let herself stall too long so the decision would be made for her.

Is that why she went to the university this morning with Taylor, not to find out if Twister was the woman in the cab, but to kill time so she could avoid the decision of whether to dig up the scroll?

Noon would come.

Whatever was destined to happen would happen.

She rationalized that she wasn't the one threatening to hurt Taylor, the so-called client was the one doing it. Although that was true, it didn't make her feel any cleaner.

She'd given Taylor a warning that the man had her in his crosshairs.

Wasn't that enough?

No it wasn't.

But the scroll had a hold on her.

It made her stall.

Why?

How?

She ended up in the financial district, soaking up the buzz. The air smelled like a combination of diesel, bar carpet and French fries. Lots of people were around, a sea of safety. No one would try to kill her in a place like this. She passed a sporting goods store, made a split-second decision and stepped inside. Ten minutes later she came out. Inside her purse, sheathed in leather, was a razor-sharp survival knife with a six-inch serrated blade and a black handle wrapped in leather.

She expected it to make her feel safer.

It did to an extent.

It also did the opposite to an extent.

One wasn't enough.

She went back and bought two more just like it, one to hide

in her apartment and the other to conceal in her office.

If the man came for her, she'd defend herself.

If he forced her to kill him, that was his choice.

76

Day Three
July 17
Thursday Morning

The shed was farther away than Wilde thought and beyond it were undeveloped spaces. Just for grins, he called to Alabama with a medium loud voice to see if she could hear him.

She couldn't.

The structure was cinderblock, windowless, the size of a half-house, with a grey shingle roof. There was a double door in the front, secured with a padlock conspicuously shinier than it should be.

"Nicole!"

No answer.

He pounded on the door.

"Nicole! Are you in there?"

Silence.

He pounded again, harder, and then put his ear to the door.

He heard nothing.

He felt no vibrations.

She either wasn't there or was unconscious.

He needed to get inside.

Right now.

This second.

The padlock was of a high quality and the doors were solid. A quick walk around the perimeter showed no windows or mortar weaknesses. He muscled onto the roof and found it strong and intact. Alabama must have seen him fussing around because she was walking towards him.

He sat down in the shade and took his hat off.

His suit was a mess.

He'd probably have to throw it away.

"You got something?" Alabama asked.

"This would be the perfect place to keep someone captive for a couple of days, don't you think?"

Alabama eyed it.

"From inside, you could shout and nobody would hear you even ten feet away," she said.

Wilde showed her the new lock.

"There's no way in," he said.

Alabama walked around the structure, returned to the front and said, "You could always take the door off the hinges."

Damn.

She was right.

The hinges were on the outside.

All he had to do was pop the pins out.

He kissed her, smack on the lips.

Then he used a rock and stick to pop the pins. He pulled the hinge-side of the door far enough out to let his body pass through and entered. The flashlight showed the interior to be one large space.

Nicole wasn't there.

A pungent odor of urine permeated the air.

"What was this, a bathroom or something?" Alabama said.

No.

There was no plumbing.

No sinks.

No toilets.

"What you're smelling is the remnants of someone who was kept here," Wilde said.

"Who?"

"My guess is Jessica Dent," he said. "The smell's been here a while. It's not recent."

Alabama wrinkled her forehead.

"You expect me to believe that you can tell new pee from old pee?"

Yes.

He did.

"What's your experience, exactly?" she asked.

"Just trust me, I can tell."

They examined every square inch with the flashlights. "Hey, I might have something," Alabama said.

Wilde looked to where she indicated, on the back wall.

The letters JD had been smudged onto the cinderblock with some type of brown substance, probably blood.

"What do you think?" Alabama asked.

"I think JD stands for Jessica Dent," he said.

His heart raced.

"Keep looking around," he said. "Maybe she wrote the guy's name in here somewhere. If we find the word *Raven*, we're done."

77

Day Three
July 17
Thursday Afternoon

Danton shadowed Night Neveraux's house for over two hours before the vehicle in the driveway, presumably Night's, finally disappeared. He didn't know if both women left but at least one had. He approached the house from the back alley.

The back door was locked.

So were the windows.

He stepped into the cover of a dilapidated wooden shed and threw a fist-sized rock through the window.

The noise was deafening but no faces appeared inside.

No neighbors craned their necks or shouted.

He took a deep breath, walked at a brisk pace to the window and slipped inside, finding himself inside a bedroom. He began searching, quickly, tearing things apart, not caring that the search would be evident. Within ten minutes he had scoured the whole house and found nothing.

Damn it.

He walked out the back door towards the alley, getting out

while the getting was good, when the falling-down wooden shack caught his eye.

No one would hide anything valuable in there.

The door had a lock but it was nothing.

He knocked it off with a rock.

Inside was a rusty lawnmower, a rake with bent fingers, an old lawn chair, assorted junk, a shovel with half the handle broken off, and more junk.

He inspected the shovel.

The break was new, not discolored like the rest of the wood.

The spade was rusty, but lots of the rust had been scraped off, particularly at the tip, suggesting recent use. He pulled the junk to the side and found freshly dug dirt.

He dug.

A foot down, he found a black bag, the kind a doctor would use.

He opened it.

Inside were jewels and valuables.

"Bingo."

He closed it up, shoved it under his arm and got the hell out of there.

The air was hot, especially after the digging.

He didn't care.

He felt great.

His thoughts turned to Ying and the drunken sex last night. That was something he could get used to. He'd played around and had his fun, still was having fun in fact. But it might not be a bad idea to settle down and see what the world looked like from the other side.

Denver wouldn't be an option though.

There was already too much baggage here—Michael Spencer and Kent Dawson, for starters. If Ying didn't want to move to Paris, maybe they could settle in San Francisco.

Yeah, that was it.

San Francisco.

78

Day Three
July 17
Thursday Afternoon

Noon came and went. Yardley paced up and down in her office with the door closed but not locked. She had a knife strategically hidden in the top drawer of her desk and another behind the planter by the window. So far, no one had shown up to kill her.

She dialed the law firm and asked for Taylor.

"She hasn't come back yet from lunch."

Yardley looked at her watch—2:12 p.m.

"Are you sure?"

Yes.

She was.

It had started.

Damn it.

It had actually started.

Taylor was a time slave, absolutely insistent on clocking at least forty billables each and every week. She usually took only 45 minutes for lunch and almost never more than an hour.

"Is Stephen Zipp in?"

"Hold on." A beat, then, "He's out of the office this afternoon in meetings."

"Okay, thanks."

What to do?

Her heart raced.

She should have just gone and gotten the scroll the minute she had the chance.

Suddenly the phone rang.

Be Taylor.

"Hello?"

Silence.

"Is anyone there?"

No response.

Then the connection died.

79

Day Three
July 17
Thursday Afternoon

There had been hotter summers but not many. Wilde took his hat off, wiped the sweat off his forehead and looked around for one more building to search.

It wasn't there.

They'd searched every nook and hideaway that this part of the world had to offer.

Nicole was nowhere to be found.

He looked at Alabama and said, "You're dying of thirst."

"Maybe a little," she said. "But I can keep going."

Wilde shook his head.

"We'll stake out Raven tonight and let him lead us to her," he said.

"So we're leaving?"

Yes.

They were.

On the way to the car, Wilde did something he didn't expect, namely swung by the cinderblock shack for one final look. He'd already put the door back on the hinges and wasn't in the mood to mess with it again.

He walked around the structure, looking carefully at the ground, then sat down on a board on the shady side. Alabama sat next to him and put her arm around his shoulders.

They didn't talk.

A bark came from up the way.

Three stray dogs were trotting their way.

Alabama stood up and eyed them with suspicion.

"I don't like dogs."

"They won't hurt you."

"You don't know that," she said.

"Yes I do."

"They could be sick or something," she said. "You don't know."

"They look fine."

"They look hungry," she said. "Light one of your fireballs."

Wilde smiled.

"Those are only for friendly purposes, not for fighting."

Alabama wasn't impressed.

She reached into Wilde's front pocket, pulled out two books of matches and got ready to fire them up.

Wilde laughed then closed his eyes.

The darkness felt like water.

Cool water.

Ice water.

The dogs came straight at them. Alabama crouched behind Wilde and said, "They're going to bite."

"If they do, bite 'em back."

They were mangier than Wilde expected, nor did they swing around as he expected. Instead they stopped a step away, in position for a handout if one was coming. Wilde held his hands up and said, "Got nothing. You can eat the girl though if you want."

The dogs studied him with curious yellow eyes, then trotted away.

Alabama punched his arm.

"Not funny."

Wilde smiled.

"A little funny."

She stood up.

"Okay, I'll admit, a little funny." A beat then, "I'm going to swing around the corner and use the facilities. No peeking."

A minute later Alabama came around the corner in the process of fastening her belt and said, "Our friends found some food."

Wilde didn't care.

He pictured himself in a café with a cheeseburger and an ice-cold cherry-coke.

"Good for them," he said.

He stood up and looked into the field. The dogs were fifty yards away, gnawing on bones.

"They found bones," he said.

"Right."

"Bones of what?"

"I don't know."

Wilde headed that way.

"Let's have a look."

"Are you crazy?"

"Come on," he said. "It'll only take a second."

"Don't bother a dog while it's eating," Alabama said. "That's rule one. Especially stray dogs."

Wilde smiled.

"Actually, rule one is that if you're in a position where animals might attack, always be with someone who runs slower than you."

80

Day Three
July 17
Thursday Afternoon

Ying wasn't home when Danton got back to the house, which was just the same because it gave him an opportunity to call Night Neveraux.

"It's me," he said, knowing that his French accent would tell the rest. "I found a little bag of goodies buried outside in your shed."

A beat.

"You're going to die."

"We're all going to die."

"You're going to suffer first."

"Here's the thing," Danton said. "Someone saw you coming out of Grace Somerfield's yard Saturday night. They gave your license plate number to the police. So far they haven't arrested you, but we both know that will be coming if—for example—they got an anonymous call that the little bag of goodies was in your house and, low and behold, they actually find them when they come over to look."

"That won't work."

"Why not?"

"Because you'd have to plant them here first," she said. "You'd die in the process."

Danton frowned.

"So dramatic," he said. "We both know you can't stay home forever. We don't have to get to that point though. The goodies are interesting and probably worth a fortune but to tell you the truth I don't really care about them. You can have them back."

Silence.

"Did you hear me? You can have them back."

"I heard you."

"And?"

"And what do you want in exchange?"

He exhaled.

"Hardly anything."

"Don't play games."

"Just one small thing."

"Go on."

"I'm going to ask you a simple question and I want an honest answer," he said. "I'm serious about what I just said. If you don't give me an honest answer then I'm going to hang up and things are going to get real bad for you. Do you understand?"

A beat.

"Go on."

"The woman who stuck the knife in my back, the Mediterranean woman, she's from Greece, am I correct?"

"That's right."

"She's in Denver to kill Emmanuelle Martin, correct?"

"Among other things."

"*Among other things*," Danton repeated. "Of course. I want to talk to her, alone, somewhere public, somewhere we'll both be safe, tonight. If things go the way I want at that meeting, you'll get your jewels back. You go your way and I go mine. Sound fair?"

"I have no power over her."

"Suit yourself."

He was hanging up when a muffled sound came from the receiver. "Suppose she meets with you," Night said. "When do I get the bag back?"

"Tonight," he said. "You won't get everything in there, though. I'm going to keep a couple of things for insurance."

Silence.

"Where do you want her to meet you?"

Good question.

"Corner of California and 16th, 9:45 p.m. Don't do anything stupid between now and then like try to kill me."

"Fine, we'll wait until afterwards."

He smiled.

"A sense of humor. I like that."

He hung up, hopped in the car and took off with the bag on the passenger seat.

He needed a safe place to stash it.

A place that wasn't Ying's house.

81

Day Three
July 17
Thursday Afternoon

It was time to break the scroll's hold on her, that's all there was to it, no matter how hard it would be. Yardley had let herself stall past the noon hour to avoid deciding whether to give it up. Now, something might have happened to Taylor, something that Yardley could have avoided if she'd been stronger. She wouldn't make the same mistake for another minute longer. She needed to get the scroll back in hand and then do with it whatever needed to be done.

She was heading out the door when her phone rang.

Stephen Zipp's voice came through.

"Rebecca said you called," he said, referring to the receptionist.

"I was calling for Taylor then thought I'd say hello to you as long as I was on the line. Is Taylor back yet?"

"Not as of five minutes ago when I walked by her office. Why?"

A pause.

She was half tempted to tell him.

The burden was so solitary.

Instead she said, "No reason. Can I ask you for a really big favor?"

"Sure."

"Can I borrow your car for an hour or two?"

"I would but it's in the shop."

"Oh, okay."

"You can borrow my motorcycle if you want."

Yardley had never ridden a motorcycle but she'd ridden a bike and a motorcycle was basically a bike with a motor.

"Okay," she said.

She swung by her apartment to get something to dig with plus her oversized purse to carry the scroll in. The place was trashed. Someone had broken in since she'd left this morning.

Who?

Taylor's client?

Her client?

Blanche Twister?

Someone hired by one of the above?

Someone new altogether?

A half hour later she was on Stephen Zipp's 1951 Indian Brave, all black except for big yellow fenders and a matching gas tank, heading south. The bike was loud, shaky and insanely more dangerous than a bicycle, but so far she'd managed to not kill herself.

She didn't have a helmet.

Her hair flew.

So did the oversized purse draped over her shoulder.

She went slowly.

Cars passed.

Someone was tearing her office apart right now, she could feel it.

Was Taylor already dead?

It took forever but she finally reached the service road at the railroad tracks, where she pulled over to catch her breath. The ground was uneven. She'd need to go slow.

A flock of geese flew overhead.

There must be water nearby.

Her face was gritty and dripping with sweat.

She wiped it off with the back of her hand.

"Okay, let's do this."

She put the bike into first and took off, wondering if Michael Spencer's body was still down there tucked into the rabbit brush. She hoped not. Seeing it last time with the bugs crawling over his eyes was enough to last her for a while.

Damn it.

There it was, up ahead, a dark shadow where a dark shadow shouldn't be. As she got closer something happened she didn't expect, there were two bodies there.

She pulled over, shut the bike down and got off.

Her legs wobbled.

The new body belonged to a man who'd been badly beaten. His left eye was mutilated beyond belief, almost as if he'd been stabbed in it. Blood, now dried to a blackish brown, covered his face.

Yardley nudged his head with her foot so she could see the other side, which was much cleaner.

She'd seen that face before.

Where?

Then it struck her.

He was the man who came into Spencer's house while she

was in there. He was the one she hid from in the bathroom tub. He was the one she saw when he looked up after jumping from the window. He was the one who made a threatening phone call to someone named Danton.

Danton must have killed him.

Since the guy was dumped with Spencer, Danton must have been the one who killed Spencer too.

The air was quiet with death.

Yardley took one last look at the bodies then turned and got on the bike. Just as she was about to crank over the engine, a noise came in the far distance behind her.

She turned to see a car speeding her way, throwing up a wild tail of dust.

She fired the bike up, shifted into first and let the clutch out. Too fast.

The bike jerked for a foot, then the engine died.

82

Day Three
July 17
Thursday Afternoon

The bones behind the shed were human. The flesh was gone, first eaten off by critters then picked clean by insects. The skull was there as were some of the other bones, but most had been carried off over time. Scraps of torn clothes were here and there, nothing more than ripped, filthy rags at this point.

Wilde picked one up and shook the dirt off.

It was a remnant of a shirt or blouse.

The buttons were on the left side, indicating a blouse.

He scraped around in the dirt, looking for anything that might indicate who the body belonged to.

Alabama spotted something half buried and pulled it out.

"It's a necklace," she said.

It was a cheap thing, once copper or brass, now corroded green.

"Hold on," Alabama said. She pulled the photo out of her back pocket, the photo from Jessica Dent's suitcase. "Got a match," she said, pointing to woman on the left. "It's the same necklace."

"So, this is Constance Black," Wilde said.

"It sure looks that way."

"I told you before I already knew she was dead," he said. "To tell you the truth, I was hoping I was wrong." He kicked the dirt. "It's pretty clear this is Warner Raven's handiwork."

"That'd be my guess," Alabama said.

"The question is, *Why?* What did he have against these women that pushed him all the way to murder?"

Alabama shook her head.

"That's not the question," she said.

Oh?

No?

Then what was the question?"

"The question is, *What are we going to do about it?*"

Wilde pulled his hat off and wiped sweat from his forehead. "I don't know," he said. "All I know is that I need to get out of the sun." He took one last look at the bones and said, "Leave the necklace here."

Alabama tossed it where she found it and matted it in with her shoe.

Then they left.

On the walk back to the MG, Wilde replayed Nicole singing at the club, barely audible over the beating of his drums, but loud enough to completely captivate him.

He needed to hear that singing again.

He needed it today.

He needed it now.

"Are you okay?"

The words came from Alabama who was staring at him with a concerned face.

"We need to find Nicole," he said.

She nodded.

"I know. Like you said, we'll stake him out tonight. He's got to visit her at least once a day."

Wilde grunted.

"If she's alive."

"He won't kill her until Friday," Alabama said.

83

Day Three
July 17
Thursday Afternoon

Danton ended up on the east side of the city in an old ghost district cluttered with dilapidated buildings and decayed streets. He drove around until he found one he liked, which was an eerie structure four or five stories tall. All the doors were either bolted, locked, or welded shut but he was able to enter through a side window.

Inside it was pitch-black, even in the day.

He felt his way to a stairwell and climbed to the top floor.

There he found a ladder that went up a hatchway to the roof. He opened the hatch, let the light splash into the structure and scouted around.

Machines, cabinets and hoists had been stripped of everything valuable and their guts had been abandoned in place. In the back corner of the floor was a room labeled Electrical. There was a steel door with a padlock hinge but no lock in place. Danton opened the door and stepped in. There was just enough light for him to make out wires dangling loose out of junction boxes.

He jiggled a couple to see if they were live.

They weren't.

The space was bigger than he anticipated, three or four meters in each direction. A metal cabinet lined the back wall. Dusty junk cluttered the shelves. The top of the cabinet went almost to the ceiling but not quite, leaving a gap of a foot or so.

Danton put the bag on the top of the cabinet and pushed it all the way back until it hit the wall.

Even if the room was lit, no one would be able to see it.

Good enough.

He closed the roof hatch and then made his way back down to the first floor where he stuck his head out the window to make sure no one was around.

No one was.

He climbed out, got in the car and headed for Ying's.

84

Day Three
July 17
Thursday Afternoon

The Indian thrashed and bucked and did its best to throw Yardley into the air as it sped over ruts and deteriorated road. She gripped the handlebars with all she had and hugged the gas tank with her legs.

The car was closing.

She put an even more serious twist on the throttle. The bike responded but jerked so violently and out of control that she had to ease off.

Who was in the car?

What did they want?

Maybe she should just pull over before she broke her body, they were going to catch her sooner or later anyway.

No.

No.

Keep going.

She turned her head just long enough to see the silhouette of a man in the vehicle, a silhouette with a hat. She didn't get enough focus to tell if he was Taylor's client, but he had the same general size and shape.

He was going to ram her then run over her when she fell. She'd end up dead or paralyzed.

Get away.

Get away.

Get away.

A new noise intersected the revving of the engine and the pounding of the bike. It was a deep, throaty, heavy noise. She looked in that direction and saw the source, a train rumbling down the tracks in her direction. She made a split-second decision and jerked the bike to the left, off the road, into a ditch and then up the embankment towards the tracks, intent on getting to the other side.

When she got to the top, the bike shot into the air and twisted violently to the left.

A landing was impossible.

She screamed and held onto the handlebars as her body catapulted off the seat.

The Indian crashed hard.

Metal twisted.

The world jerked with a surreal violence.

Pain came as she hit the ground.

Hard pain.

Serious pain.

When her body came to rest it was pinned under the front of the bike. The rear wheel was off the ground, pointed diagonally into the air, still being driven by the engine at a frantic speed. The chain cycled violently no more than a few inches from her face.

She tried to pull free.

The bike didn't budge.

An insanely loud horn filled the air.

Yardley twisted her head and saw she was in the middle of the tracks.

The train was coming at her.

It wouldn't be able to stop in time.

She closed her eyes and screamed.

85

Day Three
July 17
Thursday Afternoon

B ack at the office pacing back and forth in front of the windows, Constance Black's skull and bones shadowed Wilde's every thought. He couldn't get them out of his brain. He pictured her captive in the shed day after day and then unceremoniously taken into the field and murdered. She knew why she was being paraded out there even if Raven was making up an excuse and telling her otherwise.

That's the kind of thing a person could feel.

How did she die?

Was she stabbed?

Shot?

Smashed in the back of the head with a rock?

In hindsight, he wished he had studied the skull closer.

Tonight he'd follow Raven.

Before, he wasn't sure what he'd do if the man led him to another captive, particularly if that captive was Nicole.

Now he knew.

He would punch him in the face harder than hard. Where

it all went from there would be beyond his control. He'd take it all the way though, if that's where it went. The world would be a better place. Afterwards he'd have to decide whether to make a police report or silently mask his involvement. After all, no one knew he was working for Raven except Alabama and Nicole.

They could be trusted.

Late afternoon, the office door opened and Raven walked in. Wilde's instinct was to grab his throat and say, *Tell me where Nicole is, right this second!*

He forced it down.

If he gave up the fact that he knew what Raven was up to, the man would cover his tracks. He'd move Nicole to a different place, either that or he'd slip her into the trunk of his car, drive to some remote part of New Mexico and murder her in an arroyo, never to be found except by vultures.

He stood up and shook the man's hand.

"Good to see you."

Raven's face was somber.

"There's a rumor out on the street that you're sneaking around in my shadows," he said.

The words shocked Wilde.

He had no idea he'd been spotted.

"What do you mean?"

Raven didn't sit down. "What I mean is that assistant of yours has been asking questions about me all over town."

Wilde nodded.

"That's true."

"Why?"

"We're trying to find out who hates you enough to kill you," Wilde said. "You said yourself that you've been through all your cases and couldn't find anyone. That led me to believe that maybe it was someone from your personal life."

Raven narrowed his eyes.

"I would have told you something like that," he said.

"Maybe it's someone you don't know about."

"I would know," he said. "What do you have so far, other than investigating me?"

Wilde frowned.

"Not much, I'm afraid."

Raven headed for the door, then turned as he opened it and said, "It was a mistake hiring you. Keep the money but you're off the case. Stay out of my life. I have a reputation to maintain."

He walked out.

The door slammed.

Wilde set a book of matches on fire and let them burn down to his fingers before throwing them out the window. Alabama walked in two minutes later with two cups of coffee, handed one to Wilde and said, "You almost set me on fire down there on the sidewalk."

He took a sip.

It was like medicine.

It would keep him up tonight.

He told her about Raven's visit.

"It's my fault," Alabama said. "I should have been more discrete."

The words weren't just words.

She really meant them.

Wilde gave her a hug and said, "There's no way you could have done it better." He took a sip and added, "Things are going to be tricky from this point on. He'll be watching for us."

"He came here for verification, right?"

Wilde nodded.

Right.

"And I gave it to him."

"He wouldn't move Nicole until he got that verification, right?"

Probably not.

"He might move her now though, even before dark," she said. "Do you think we should get back out to the warehouses?"

Wilde raised an eyebrow.

"How much am I paying you?"

She shrugged.

"I don't know. You never told me."

"Well, whatever it was, you just got a raise." He pulled the gun out of the drawer and stuck it in his waistband. "Let's go."

86

Day Three
July 17
Thursday Afternoon

Ying still wasn't home when Danton got back, so he lathered up in the shower to wash the dead-building grime off his skin. He stepped out naked toweling his hair to find a woman sitting on the sofa, a woman who wasn't Ying, a woman who was the last person he expected to see—Emmanuelle.

She ran her eyes down his body.

He froze.

Then he continued drying off without covering up.

"You gave me the number," Emmanuelle said. "I called earlier this afternoon and spoke to your girlfriend. She gave me the address. Here I am."

"Right, here you are."

She walked over, wrapped her arms around him and kissed the stitches on his chest.

"These are from me," she said.

True.

They were.

"I'm sorry."

She went over to her purse, pulled a knife out and handed it to him.

"I'm here to pay my debt."

Danton moved his hand up and down, getting a feel for the weight of the knife.

"You want me to stab you?"

"To be honest, I'm hoping you don't," she said. "But it's your choice."

Danton picked her off her feet, slammed her on the carpet on her back and straddled her.

She didn't resist.

He waved the knife back and forth in front of her face.

"I've thought about killing you a hundred times," he said.

She stared into his eyes.

"Do it."

Danton ripped open her blouse and tore her bra off. Then he ran the tip of the blade down her chest, deep enough to draw a line of blood. Half his brain told him to raise his arm as high as it would go and slam the knife into her chest with every ounce of strength he had. The other half told him to rip her pants off and take her.

He did neither.

Instead he threw the knife across the room.

Then he licked the blood off her chest.

87

Day Three
July 17
Thursday Afternoon

The ground shook and vibrated from the horrific weight of the approaching train. The engineer pulled the whistle, again and again and again. Yardley pushed against the bike with every ounce of strength she had.

It didn't budge.

She pushed again.

It didn't move.

In ten seconds she'd be dead.

The whistle blew.

This was it.

She pushed with all her might. The bike didn't move, not an inch, but then it shifted, almost imperceptibly, but some. She pushed harder. Suddenly the back wheel contacted the ground and the bike shot off, across the track and down the embankment.

The train was right on her.

She didn't have time to stand.

She rolled.

Then more.

She snagged on the rail.

Then she pushed over.

The engine passed so close that a vacuum almost sucked her under. She rolled harder, hoping beyond hope that nothing would catch her.

Then she was free.

Rolling down the embankment.

Free.

Free.

Free.

She got to her feet and could see the car through the clanking wheels.

It was stopped.

She ran in the field with one thought and one thought only, to get as far of a head start as she could while the train protected her. Within a dozen steps she realized it wouldn't work.

Pain came from her knee.

She could hardly bend her leg.

She looked around for a place to hide.

There were no trees or structures or ground swells or anything of significance, not as far as she could see in any direction.

Damn it.

Damn it.

Damn it.

She was trapped.

88

Day Three
July 17
Thursday Afternoon

Wilde lit a book of matches as he headed down the stairs, then threw them on the sidewalk at ground level. The MG was parked a half-block down. As he and Alabama headed that way, they saw a man in a suit standing in front of it, writing down the license plate number. His face was tough, a Camel dangled from his lips, a scar ran across his chin.

"Can I help you?" Wilde said.

"Is this yours?"

"Yes."

"Are you Bryson Wilde?"

"Yes."

"Do you know someone named Night Neveraux?"

Wilde tilted his head.

"Who's asking?"

The man pulled a badge.

"Johnny Pants, homicide."

"Who's dead?"

"Grace Somerfield."

"You're heading that up?"

"I'm on the team," he said. "I'm going to get right to the point. A green MG was seen leaving the alley behind Night Neveraux's house just as we showed up to search it. Was that you?"

Wilde considered denying it but didn't have time to play out all the twists. It would be safer to tell the truth.

"Yes."

"The word is that you squealed out pretty fast. Were you taking anything with you, something that maybe Night Neveraux gave you to take?"

"Like what?"

"Oh, I don't know. Maybe something like items that came out of Grace Somerfield's vault."

Wilde swallowed and appeared to not be affected.

"I don't know what you're talking about."

Pants cocked his head.

"Accessory after the fact is a serious crime," he said. "It's a felony. It could land you in jail for a long, long time. I'm going to forget the answer you just gave me and make things as easy for you as I can if you tell me the truth. So let me ask it again. Did you make off with those items when we showed up to search the house?"

"No."

"No?"

"No."

Pants exhaled.

"Have it your way," he said. "At some point in the future you'll look back at this moment and wish you could redo it. Are you positive about your answer?"

"Yes."

Pants frowned.

"Do you mind if I search your office?"

"What for?"

Pants shrugged.

"Just for grins."

"Yes."

"Yes I can search it or yes you mind?"

"Yes I mind."

"Why, do you have something to hide?"

Wilde walked past, close enough to brush him back, and got in the car.

"Unless you have a warrant, we're done here," he said.

"I guess we are, for now," Pants said. "I'll be in touch."

"You do that." Wilde cranked over the engine and shifted into first but didn't take off. "Who's in charge of the Somerfield investigation?"

"You don't read the newspapers?"

"Apparently not."

"Warner Raven," Pants said.

"Warner Raven."

"Right, Warner Raven. Do you know him?"

"I've heard the name."

"You'll probably hear it again," Pants said, patting the hood of the car. "Be careful in this thing. It's a death trap. You meet a Chevy head on and you're deader than dead."

"I'll keep that in mind."

"It doesn't even have a front bumper," Pants added.

"That's because the people that drive them know how to watch where they're going."

Wilde tipped his hat and pulled off with a racing heart.

"Damn that was close," Alabama said. "Do you think Raven's behind it?"

Wilde nodded.

"I'm just surprised it started so quickly."

Alabama patted his knee.

"Can we trust Night?" she asked.

"I hope so."

"You're not sure?"

"Nothing's sure when it comes to Night." A beat, then, "They'll arrest me Friday afternoon, if not earlier. You too, if my hunch is right, as an accessory to an accessory or some such bullshit. That way Raven gets a double whammy, namely he gets us off the streets and also discredits us. We can shout up and down all we want about him murdering Jessica Dent but all anyone will see is someone trying to wiggle their way out of being caught in connection with Grace Somerfield's murder."

"I don't think he's going to arrest us," Alabama said.

Wilde turned to see if she was serious.

She was.

"You don't think so?"

"No," she said. "I think he's going to kill us in the process of the arrest, you know, say we were resisting or something like that. He'll plant guns on us."

Wilde chewed on it.

It was plausible.

"You want out?"

Alabama laughed.

"All this does is want to make me be further in."

"In that case you're crazier than I am."

"No, not crazier. As crazy, but not crazier. No one's crazier."

He smiled.

"Nice of you to notice."

89

Day Three
July 17
Thursday Afternoon

D anton couldn't convince Emmanuelle to pack her bags and get out of Denver even though there was now a second hit woman—a Greek staying with Night Neveraux—after her.

"I need to see this through," she said.

Danton paced.

"You won't live to see it through."

"That's my problem, not yours."

"Let me handle it," Danton said. "You're good at what you do but you're out of your league at this point. Just cut yourself loose and vanish."

"I can't."

"Why not?"

"Because I let you down," she said.

"Don't worry about it."

"How can you say that after what I did?"

He shrugged.

"It's in the past."

She studied him.

"Are you aware that I killed Zeno Leva?" she asked.

Danton stopped in mid-pace.

"Are you serious?"

Yes.

She was.

"Why?" Danton asked.

"Same reason I tried to kill you," she said. "He was a loose end."

Danton shook his head.

"You were never like this before," he said. "What happened?"

She exhaled.

"I don't know." The buttons were gone from her blouse, not to mention the bloodstains. "Do you think your girlfriend will mind if I borrow something from her closet?"

Danton shook his head and pointed.

"That way."

She stepped into the bathroom, got a towel wet and wiped the blood off her chest. The cut was long and tender but had stopped bleeding. Then she found a black T-shirt in a dresser drawer and put it on.

"I have a lead I'm going to run down tonight," she said, heading for the door.

"Where are you staying?"

She hesitated, deciding, then said, "The Kenmark. I'll be in touch." She was halfway out the door when she stopped and turned. "Just for the record, trying to kill you was the hardest thing I've ever done in my life. Do you know why?"

He shook his head.

No.

Why?

"Because I'd let myself do something I swore I'd never let myself do," she said. "I let myself fall in love with you."

Then she left.

90

Day Three
July 17
Thursday Afternoon

Yardley was trapped. The train would pass and then she'd be murdered. She pushed down the pain coming from her knee and scouted around frantically. There was nowhere to hide, nowhere to go.

The motorcycle was on its side thirty steps away, now quiet and dead.

Wait.

Did it still run?

She got over to it, muscled it upright and swung her leg over the seat.

Come on, baby, start!

She turned the key.

The engine sputtered but didn't catch.

She turned it again.

This time it caught.

She shifted into first and headed into the open space as the final car of the train passed by. The front tire wobbled and rubbed against the forks. A terrible noise came from the rear sprocket.

Don't fall off.

Don't fall off.

She turned her head just long enough to see if the man was running after her.

He was.

She twisted the throttle and hung on for all she was worth.

Rot in hell, asshole.

91

Day Three
July 17
Thursday Night

Wilde and Alabama took every precaution to not be spotted, including parking the MG a mile away at the South Platte and hoofing to the warehouse district on foot, together with claiming a stakeout of the area from the roof of the building Wilde inspected last night, the one with the blood on the floor.

It did no good.

Warner Raven didn't show up.

All remained quiet.

At seven they gave up and headed home for food and a shower. Wilde stuck a dozen fresh packs of matches in his shirt pocket and another twenty or so in his suit. Alabama looked at him sideways, then pulled them out and put them on the table.

"Has Raven ever seen your nasty little habit?"

A beat.

"Yes."

"If he sees something like that tonight, do you think he'll figure out it's you?"

Wilde put two in his shirt pocket.

"Just for security," he said. "We need a different car. That MG sticks out too much."

"It'll be dark," Alabama said.

"It doesn't matter, the headlights are too close together."

He called Night.

"Can we trade cars for tonight?"

"I have a meeting," she said. "I can't be without wheels."

"You'll have the MG."

"The steering wheel's on the wrong side."

"So?"

"So, I can't shift with my left hand."

"Yeah you can."

"Trust me, I'll end up chewing up your gears."

It took two minutes of convincing but she finally relented.

There.

Done.

Alabama wasn't impressed. "Night killed Grace Somerfield and will go down for it sooner or later. Tangling up with her is the last thing you should be doing."

Wilde didn't care.

"All I care about is getting Nicole back."

Shortly after dark they swung by Raven's house.

He was home.

Good.

They took up a position down the street and waited.

They waited a full hour, then Raven's headlights popped on and headed into the night. Wilde followed with the gun on the seat.

"This is it," he said.

He expected to be pulled east into the warehouse district

but the vehicle headed north.

"Where's he going?"

"I don't know."

They followed without talking for a mile, then another, then another. Alabama suddenly groaned and said, "Don't look at the fuel gauge."

Wilde did.

It was almost on E.

92

Day Three
July 17
Thursday Night

Ten minutes before the appointed time Thursday night, Danton took a position in the shadows down California Street where he could see to the corner, then waited for the Mediterranean woman to show up.

The night was dark.

The insane heat of the day was gone.

The air was comfortable. His palms shouldn't be sweating but they were. When he closed his eyes he could feel the point of the woman's knife in his back.

She'd try to kill him tonight.

That was certain.

It wouldn't be immediately, though. First she'd hear what he had to say. She'd try to get him to tell her where the bag of goodies was. Ying was in the Packard parked a block north, waiting to be his getaway if he needed it. Danton told her everything that happened today, including Emmanuelle showing up out of the blue and her announcement that she loved him.

Ying laughed.

"I'm sorry," she said. "But if you love someone, you don't kill them."

Danton shrugged.

"She's complicated."

"What does that mean, that you actually believe her?"

"To tell you the truth, I'm not all that interested in it one way or the other. It turns out that I've met someone."

Ying rubbed her breasts on his chest.

"Oh yeah? Who?"

"Just a woman," he said. "She's about your height."

"My height, huh? My weight, too?"

He ran his eyes down her body.

"Now that you mention it, yes."

"Does she look anything like me?"

"Actually, you could be twins."

"Lucky woman," Ying said.

"I haven't told her yet," he said. "I'm not sure how she'll take it."

"You should tell her someday and find out."

He kissed her.

"Maybe I will."

He looked at his watch—9:40 p.m.

Five minutes.

Just five more minutes.

He hardened his heart, narrowed his eyes and wiped his palms on his pants. There were headlights coming up and down the streets but not nearly as many as he envisioned. At some point the woman would have a clear opportunity to kill him.

She was trained.

She'd done it before.

Probably dozens of times.

Don't let her get too close.

Keep an eye on her hands.

Don't let them disappear behind her back or inside a jacket.

93

When Yardley looked behind for that brief heart-beat as she pounded into the field on the Indian, she got just enough of a glimpse at the man chasing her to be 98 percent sure he was Taylor's "client," the man who had given them a noon deadline to return the scroll.

Unfortunately for him, his car couldn't follow.

Yardley escaped then laid low at a fleabag hotel, nervously peeking out from behind the blinds all afternoon with the motorcycle parked out back, venturing out only to call Stephen and confess what she'd done to his poor Indian—which she would pay for, every cent. She also called the firm a half dozen times to see if Taylor had shown up yet.

She hadn't.

One thing became clear as the seconds ticked by; if Taylor was still alive, there was only one way for Yardley to find her, and that was to get the client to take her there. She wanted to hide, she wanted to disappear, but those weren't options. After dark, she took a cab back to the city, quietly climbed up the fire escape of her building and looked in her windows.

No one was inside.

She climbed back down, entered through the door and kept the lights off. Under the bed sheet, she stuffed clothes in the shape of a sleeping body.

In the living room, she pulled the couch away from the wall until she got a gap big enough to lay her body in.

Then she laid down on her back with a knife in her hand.

"Come on, asshole. Come for me."

94

Day Three
July 17
Thursday Night

Raven wound farther and farther north out of the city into increasingly thinner traffic. Wilde shifted his body in search of a more comfortable position and said, "He's going to spot us if he hasn't already."

"Turn here," Alabama said.

"Why?"

"Trust me."

Wilde made a right.

"Turn your lights off and get back on him," she said.

"That's too dangerous."

"So is running with scissors," she said. "Do it."

Wilde did it. They lost distance but made it up fairly quickly. "If he spots a car without headlights that will be a dead give-away."

"He won't," Alabama said. "He can only spot headlights."

Wilde gave her a sideways glance.

Five minutes later Raven pulled in front of a greasy spoon with a partially burned out neon sign that should have said

Restaurant but said Rest Ant. Wilde stopped short and watched Raven head inside, where the man slipped into a booth with another man.

Wilde pulled up closer, still with the lights out.

The other man's face came into focus.

It was the detective from the MG, the one who wanted to search Wilde's office.

Johnny Pants.

"I don't like the looks of this," Wilde said. "What are those two doing hooking up after hours?"

"Probably talking about you," Alabama said.

Wilde knew it was a joke but there was too much ugly truth to laugh.

"I'm going to do something and I don't want you to try to stop me," Alabama added.

"No."

"No what?"

"No, don't do it."

"You don't even know what it is," Alabama said.

"I don't have to," Wilde said. "If it's something where you warn me not to stop you, it's already something I don't like."

She smiled.

"Don't you want to know what it is?"

"No."

"Good, because here it is," she said. "I'm going to slip into the backseat of Raven's car and hide on the floor. That way when he heads to wherever he's going, I'll know where he went, even if you end up getting lost."

Wilde reached for her arm but she was already out the door.

She blew him a kiss and said, "Wish me luck."

Wilde had his hand on the handle to go after her when an image of Nicole popped in his head, an image of her tied up in some dark hole, desperate and alone, preparing herself to die on Friday.

The image froze his hand.

He exhaled as Alabama crept to the passenger side of Raven's car and slipped inside.

"Don't lose her," Wilde told himself. "Don't you dare lose her."

One minute later Raven came out of the Rest Ant walking fast. He got in the vehicle, backed up, then came south directly at Wilde.

95

Day Three
July 17
Thursday Night

At exactly 9:45 a car with a blond driver pulled to the curb at the corner of California and 16th. The Mediterranean woman stepped out and the car took off.

Game time.

Danton headed that way and stopped a yard away, just out of reach. The woman had nothing in her hands. She wore black pants and a black blouse, semi-baggy.

Loose enough to hide a gun or a knife.

"You wanted to meet, here I am," she said.

"I want you to deliver a message to Petracca," he said. "Tell him we're sorry about his wife. No one was supposed to get hurt. Tell him that neither me nor Emmanuelle had a gun on the night in question. Zeno Leva was the one with the gun. We didn't know he had it until he pulled it out and fired. Afterwards, Emmanuelle killed him for what he did."

"I'm sure Petracca will be touched," the woman said.

Danton ran his fingers through his hair.

"Here's the way things are going to go down," he said.

"You're going to get out of Denver. If you don't, like I said before, the police will end up finding Grace Somerfield's things in Night's house. She'll be history."

The woman's face hardened.

"Here's the way it's going to go down," she said. "I'm going to finish my mission. I'm going to kill Emmanuelle. Then I'm going to kill you. If anything ever shows up at Night's house, then there will be a third person on my list, your little slant-eyed girlfriend."

"I don't care about her."

"Then don't care. She'll still go down."

The woman walked away.

Three steps later she turned and said over her shoulder, "Have a nice evening."

When he got back to the car Ying asked, "So how'd it go?"

"Not good," he said.

"What does that mean?"

"It means she left me no choice except to do what I'm going to have to do."

A beat.

"I'll help."

"No."

"Yes."

"Why?"

She shifted into first and pulled out.

"After Spencer and Dawson, it's the least I can do."

Danton shook his head.

"It's too dangerous. She's a professional. What we need to do is get you out of town and hidden away somewhere. That will give me a chance to do things without having to worry about watching your back."

Silence.

"Did you hear me?" he asked.

She looked over.

"I'm sorry, have you been talking?"

He smiled.

"I'm serious."

"I'm not leaving your side so just get used it," she said. "When do we do it? Right now? Tonight?"

96

The shattering of a window pulled Yardley back from the edge of sleep. She held her breath, knowing something was wrong but not knowing what. Then she remembered. She was behind the couch, lying in wait with a knife in her hand.

Smaller remnants of glass got brushed off and fell to the floor.

The window unlatched.

It slid up.

A person climbed through and stood motionless.

Yardley tightened her grip on the knife. She was flat on her back, a defenseless position but one she couldn't shift out of without making noise.

Three footsteps.

That's what the intruder took.

Three footsteps.

He was in the middle of the room.

Why did he stop?

Did he notice the couch out of position?

Was he getting ready to come over and take a peek behind it, just in case someone was hiding there?

Stay quiet.

Stay quiet.

Stay quiet.

The man was fussing with something, then an odor weaved through the air, barely detectible, but something different than normal.

Suddenly the couch pulled away.

A heavy figure straddled her, pinning her arms motionless. It was a man, the client. He covered her face with a wet cloth, forcing a nasty chemical into her nose and mouth and eyes. She fought to get her face loose.

It did no good.

Suddenly the fight went out of her body.

Everything faded to black.

Her brain returned to a vague and throbbing focus at some point later, which could have been three minutes or three hours. Her body wouldn't move. Her hands were tied behind her back. Her ankles were strapped together. She pulled at her bonds, frantic. They wouldn't budge.

She pulled again, harder.

Same thing.

Her breathing was heavy and difficult, a hood was over her head, cinched around her neck.

She was somewhere dark, in something moving.

The trunk of a car?

Yes.

That was it.

Okay.

Think.

Think.

Think.

He hasn't killed you yet.

Sooner or later he'll stop and pull you out.

You're not dead yet.

Don't panic.

Get your breathing under control.

Don't hyperventilate.

The ride continued for another ten or fifteen or twenty minutes, then the vehicle came to a stop and the engine shut off. A car door opened, a foot landed on the ground, then the door slammed shut.

Footsteps came down the side of the car.

Knuckles rapped on the trunk.

"Come out, come out wherever you are."

Her instinct was to shout *Go to hell!*

Instead she went limp and pretended to be unconscious.

97

Day Three
July 17
Thursday Night

Wilde followed Raven as far back as he could, then he did one better by letting a car behind him pass, giving him a buffer. They went south, back into the guts of the city. Suddenly Raven pulled to the side of the street and the other car slid in behind him.

Wilde couldn't stop, it would be too conspicuous.

He passed, shielding his face with his hat.

The other driver turned out to be Johnny Pants.

As Wilde drove off, his rearview mirror showed Pants getting into Raven's car, which then pulled away. Wilde sped up to get a good lead, then pulled over, killed the lights and ducked down. The plan was to let them pass then get back in behind them.

Seconds passed.

Then more.

Then too many.

Raven's car didn't pass. Wilde looked up to see where it was. It was nowhere.

The headlights were gone.

They must have turned.

Damn it.

He did a one-eighty, cut left at the first cross-street and said, "Come on, be up there."

Taillights appeared.

As he got closer, they weren't Raven's. He passed and sped up.

More taillights appeared but none belonged to Raven.

The man was gone.

Alabama was on her own.

It was Wilde's fault.

He pulled to the side and smacked his fist so hard on the dash that the speedometer glass cracked.

He should have stopped Alabama.

He should have never let her do anything as stupid as what she did. He was the one in charge. Not stopping her was his fault.

Damn it.

Now what?

Drive around aimlessly and hope to bump into them by accident?

No.

Think.

Think.

Think.

Where were they headed, that was the question? If he knew where they were going, he could intercept them there.

Maybe they were going to Raven's house.

No, that didn't make sense, because why would they drop Pants' car off if that was the case? Pants would just follow him there.

Maybe they were headed to the warehouse district.

But wait, if that was the case, then Pants would be in cahoots with the murders.

There wouldn't be just one killer.

There would be two.

Wilde shifted into first and headed that way.

98

Day Three
July 17
Thursday Night

D anton and Ying drove by Night's house several times over the next hour, and even went in once, to no avail. The women weren't there. Danton cocked his head and said, "They're probably doing the same thing we are, staking out your house."

Ying smiled.

"That would be ironic."

"Wouldn't it?"

"Ships passing in the night." A beat then, "So what should we do, hole up someplace safe?"

Danton shook his head.

"Let's just go home," he said. "If they show up, they show up. The sooner the better, if you ask me."

Ying ran her fingers over the back of his neck.

"You're not afraid?"

He grunted.

"Of course I'm afraid," he said. "Don't tell anyone, though."

Back home, Danton searched the house while Ying drove around the block.

It was safe.

Inside, they locked the doors and windows and hid knives in strategic positions. Then they turned out the lights and laid down in bed with their clothes on.

"I have a painting," Ying said. "It's worth a lot of money."

"Where?"

"In the basement," she said. "It's an original Renoir."

"How'd you get it?"

"It got stolen from a museum in Paris thirty years ago," she said.

"By who?"

"I have no idea," she said. "I was thinking that we could go somewhere, lay low for a while, then sell it and live in luxury."

"Why haven't you done that already?"

"I don't know," she said. "I guess I've been too scared. To be honest, I think the painting has a curse on it. People who end up in contact with it seem to end up dead. Do you want to see it?"

He considered it.

"Let's just leave it where it is until we find out if our guests are going to show up," he said. "If they kill us, that will get me mad. If they kill us and make off with an original Renoir in the process, that would really get me mad."

Silence.

"I have no idea how to sell it," she said. "Do you?"

Danton laughed.

"Me? No, not hardly," he said. "But I know who does."

"Yeah? Who?"

"Sam Poppenberg."

He didn't have to explain. Poppenberg lived in New York. He was the one who put Danton in touch with Ying in the first place, when he needed a contact in Denver.

"He's into stolen art?"

"I doubt if he is personally, but I'm sure he knows someone who is." A beat then, "How do you know him, anyway?"

"I met him through a friend."

"Who?"

"Jessica Dent," she said. "She's the one in the picture with me in the living room, the one who got murdered." A beat then, "Did you really mean it before when you said you'd help me find out who killed her after this Emmanuelle thing got put to bed?"

He squeezed her hand.

"If that's important to you, then yes."

"It's important," she said. "Every time I think about it, I get this weird feeling that she was killed by a cop."

"Why?"

"I don't know," she said. "Maybe it's because they never seemed to come up with any evidence."

Danton exhaled.

"Who was the detective in charge of the investigation?"

"A guy named Johnny Pants."

"Weird name."

"Weird guy," Ying said. "I never liked him, not from day one."

They made slow, sweet love.

Then Danton said, "You stay here and go to sleep. I'm going to stand guard in the living room."

99

Day Three
July 17
Thursday Night

The trunk opened and a heavy hand smacked Yardley's ass. Strong arms pulled her out and flung her over a shoulder, feet to the front and her head dangling at the man's back. Then she was in motion, being carried.

"Stop!"

"Shut up."

"I didn't do anything."

He slapped her ass.

The sting ran up her spine into her brain.

Then he slapped her again, even harder, which forced an unintelligible noise from her mouth. She concentrated on the pain, saying nothing.

The walking continued.

Then the man stopped, yanked Yardley off his shoulder and laid her on the ground.

She felt dirt.

She smelled oil.

The man was doing something, possibly unlocking a lock,

then a heavy metal door slid open. He pulled her off the ground, carried her up a short ladder and stepped inside something.

No doubt a building of some sort.

The door slammed shut.

The man laid her back down.

The floor was cold and hard.

Her hood was ripped off. What she saw she could hardly believe. Taylor Lee was in front of her, sitting on the floor with her back against some type of metal wall. Her arms were stretched above her head and held handcuffed to some kind of protrusion. Her mouth was gagged. The man shined a flashlight up and down Taylor's body, giving Yardley a good look.

Then he shined the light into Yardley's eyes.

"Now listen carefully," he said. "Your little friend here is going to die, do you understand? She's going to die unless you give me the scroll. You have it, don't you? Admit that you have it."

A pause.

"Yes."

"I knew it," he said. "Where is it?"

"It's buried."

"We're going to go unbury it right now," he said. "As soon as I have it, you'll both go free."

Taylor shook her head negative.

The man slapped her face.

"Shut up!" Then to Yardley, "I'm not going to kill anyone so long as you cooperate. All I want is the scroll. Once I get it, we'll all go our separate ways. Do you understand?"

"Yes."

"Good."

He yanked her to her feet and put the hood back over her

head.

"Let's go."

100

Day Three
July 17
Thursday Night

Wilde parked by the South Platte and headed into the industrial area on foot. The night was blacker than black. The buildings, the sky and the earth were all smothered with the same thick pitch. He could come within thirty steps of a parked car and never know it.

Come on, Alabama.

Be here somewhere.

He picked his way towards the tallest building, the five-story job with the blood on the concrete and the shack out back, the shack where Jessica Dent lived out her last days.

What was Johnny Pants' role in all this?

Maybe Wilde had been pointed in the wrong direction all along. He'd been looking for a connection between Raven and the dead women. Maybe that connection didn't exist. Maybe the connection was between Pants and the dead women, intertwined with a second connection between Pants and Raven. Maybe Raven killed the women but did it for Pants rather than himself.

Complicated.

That's what it was, complicated.

Too complicated.

Right now he didn't have time to think about it. Right now Alabama might be getting killed. That's what he needed to stay focused on.

He carried the gun in his right hand.

The chambers were full.

The steel was hard.

He broke out of his walk into a trot, then powered the trot into a run. What he needed to see was a light, however brief, however faint, a splash of headlights or the jab of a flashlight or an orange cigarette tip, it didn't matter, just something to give him a mark.

No marks came.

The building loomed ahead, still almost invisible but taking a greater and greater definition as he approached.

No car was parked in front.

No sounds came from anywhere.

No light came from anywhere.

He trotted around the side of the structure towards the back where the shack was.

Come on, be a creature of habit.

Do the same trick twice.

Suddenly he heard a noise.

It was faint.

It almost wasn't there.

It was there enough, though, to bring him to a halt. He tried to get a bearing. His breathing was thick and heavy and drummed in his ears. He held his breath and focused.

The sound was coming from his right.

He turned his head directly at it.

Suddenly a yap split the air, something dog-like but not exactly. Then more yapping came, from three or four or five throats.

Coyotes.

Stupid coyotes.

He turned and made his way down the side of the structure, then around to the back. The shack was a hundred yards away. No sounds came from it. No lights came from it. If there was a vehicle parked in the area, Wilde couldn't see it.

He headed that way with a heavy chest.

The uneven earth twisted his ankles and the wild grasses rubbed against his pants.

Alabama wouldn't be there.

He could already tell.

101

Day Three
July 17
Thursday Night

It's buried off the service road by the railroad tracks, the ones you followed me to this afternoon." That said, Yardley was then put back in the trunk, still tied, still in the hood, until they got there. Then the car stopped, the trunk opened and she was jerked out.

The man ripped her hood off.

The night was dark.

They were on the service road.

"If you lied to me about the scroll being here, you're going to learn a very hard lesson," the man said. "Where is it?"

"It's down the road."

The man put her in the passenger seat and headed into the blackness.

"Tell me when to stop," he said.

"It's a ways."

"How far?"

"I don't know, a couple miles," she said. "We're looking for a pinion pine. That's where we need to stop."

The headlights punched eerily down the road.

There was no more desolate place on earth.

She swallowed and stole a sideways glance at the man.

The dashboard lights etched his face.

He was intense.

He looked like he was preparing to kill her.

"If I tell you where it is, you said you'd let me and Taylor go," Yardley said.

The man grunted.

"There is no *if* at this point," he said. "You're either going to tell me or you're going to fall into a hole of pain so deep and dark that you'll pee your pants a hundred times. I'm through screwing around. Get that through your head."

She stared out the window.

In ten minutes she'd be dead.

She didn't want to die.

Not out here.

Not alone.

Not like this.

It was going to happen, though. She couldn't stop it. The thought consumed her. She felt a wetness on her seat, one she hadn't noticed before, and realized that her bladder had released.

The man said, "Damn you," and slapped her head.

Tears engulfed her eyes and ran down her face.

Suddenly the pinion appeared.

"Is that it?"

She said nothing.

"I said, is that it?"

"Yes."

The man stopped at the side of the road, killed the engine and turned off the headlights.

The darkness was absolute.

Without the noise of the engine and the chafing of the tires, Yardley heard the excess of her own breathing and realized she was hyperventilating.

"Where is it?"

"It's out in the field a ways."

"Show me."

"How?"

The man reached in the glove compartment, pulled out a hunting knife and cut the ropes around Yardley's ankles. He left her arms tied behind her back, then he grabbed her by the throat and said, "Understand something right now and understand it good. If you try to run, you'll pay for it. So will your little friend. Are we clear on that?"

She nodded.

"Say it."

A beat.

"Yes.

"Yes what?"

"Yes I'm clear on it."

"Good, stay where you are."

The man got out, slammed his door shut, walked around the car and pulled Yardley out. Then he turned on a flashlight, pointed it at the ground and said, "Now show me."

"It's this way."

Yardley counted off the steps until she got to the moss rock.

"It's under that rock," she said.

"How far down?"

"Not far, a foot or so."

"It better be there," he said.

"It is."

He pushed her back a step.

"Stand right there and don't move. Do you understand?"

"Yes."

The man pushed the rock to the side and dug with the knife. The soil was loose. The flashlight laid on the ground, pointed at Yardley's feet.

She watched.

Frozen.

Two minutes.

That's all it would take before he reached the scroll.

Two more minutes.

As soon as he had it in hand, he'd shove the knife in her stomach. Then he'd go back to Taylor and do the same to her.

Poof.

All the witnesses would be gone.

The man was looking down, concentrating on the digging.

A primitive gene grabbed Yardley's brain.

She pulled her foot back and kicked it at the man's face with every ounce of strength she had.

It landed squarely, so much so that his head snapped violently and he catapulted backwards onto his spine.

"You goddamn bitch!"

Yardley ran.

Don't fall!

Don't fall!

Don't fall!

She created a gap but the man was behind her, shouting, closing the distance with each passing second. Suddenly a fist of steel grabbed her hair from behind and yanked back so hard that it snapped her entire body backwards to the ground.

The man stood over her, panting heavily.

"I told you not to run," he said. "You brought this on your-self."

She closed her eyes as the man grabbed her face.

DAY FOUR

July 18
Friday

102

Day Four
July 18
Friday Morning

Something crawled across Wilde's face. At first it registered as a sensation, neither good nor bad. As he became more and more conscious, it took on an increasingly dangerous aura. He opened his eyes to find something slithering. He frantically brushed it off to the side and twisted his head to the other. It was a rattlesnake.

He rolled as fast as he could.

The reptile curled up, raised its head and shook its tail.

Wilde got to his feet and stepped away.

He kicked dirt at it then looked around.

The first rays of dawn were seeping into the morning sky. He was in the warehouse district. Why? Then he remembered searching for Alabama for hours last night before finally collapsing on the ground to rest for a few minutes.

His stomach growled.

His tongue was sandpaper.

His clothes were filthy beyond repair.

He picked up his hat, slapped it against his leg until the dust stopped flying, then tilted it over his left eye and headed for the car.

Damn it.

No Alabama.

No Alabama all night.

He headed home, hoping against hope that she found her way back last night. He bounded through the front door and shouted, "Alabama!"

No answer came.

"Alabama!"

Nothing.

Only silence.

Damn it.

Damn it to hell.

His body ached from the relentless hours on the dirt. He grabbed a quart of orange juice from the fridge and downed it as he stripped out of his pathetic clothes. Then he got the shower up to temperature and stayed in until the hot water ran out.

He dried off, combed his wet hair straight back and slipped into a fresh suit.

Then he headed for the office.

He was getting the coffee pot fired up when the door opened and a timid woman stuck her head in. Wilde didn't know her but knew the look on her face.

It was one of fear.

One of uncertainty.

One of desperation.

It mirrored how he felt.

"Are you Bryson Wilde?"

He was.

"I really hope you can help me," she said. "I have something desperate going on."

He almost blurted out, *No.*

No way.

I'm sorry, I really am, but I already have more going on than the law allows. I don't even have time to spell new client, much less have one.

The look on her face wouldn't let his lips move in that direction though.

The look on her face made him say, "Do you want some coffee?"

She took a step inside but didn't shut the door.

"I'll pay you, whatever it is you charge, but I don't have the money right now. I'll have to save it up."

Wilde shrugged.

"Was that a *yes* on the coffee?"

She nodded.

"That would be nice."

103

Day Four
July 18
Friday Morning

Danton, still alive, picked his achy body off the living room floor as the first rays of daylight bled through the curtains. Outside everything looked normal. He picked the knife off the floor, set it on the table and headed for the bedroom. Ying was balled up under the covers snoring lightly. Danton gave her an imperceptible kiss on the check and headed for the shower.

Halfway through Ying stepped in.

"It looks like we're still alive," she said.

"It's a good thing," he said. "It's my favorite way to start the day."

She stuck her head under the spray and rubbed her face.

"Lather me up, Frenchman."

Right.

Good idea.

He ran the soap over her neck and shoulders.

She turned and rested her hands against the wall above her head and let the spray hit her face. Danton ran the soap over her underarms and breasts, then down to her incredibly taut stomach.

She wiggled her ass.

Danton rubbed against her.

Then he took her from behind.

He took her until she screamed those little screams he loved so much.

Afterwards, over coffee and waffles, he said, "I have something I want to tell you. I have money."

"I know."

"I'm not talking about money money," he said, "I'm talking about insane money. I'm talking about the kind of money that you need a math degree to count."

She studied him.

"Where'd you get all this insane money?"

He diverted his eyes, then looked at her. "I steal things. There. Now you know." A beat. "I didn't know if I'd tell you. I guess I know the answer now."

She took a sip of coffee.

"What do you steal, exactly?"

"Things worth my time."

"Things worth your time," she repeated.

He nodded.

"I want you to come to Paris with me."

She sat on his lap and ran her fingers through his hair.

"And what would I do in Paris?"

"You'd be my partner."

"Partner? I thought you were going to say lover."

"Partner includes lover," he said.

"Is that what Emmanuelle was, your partner?"

"I thought she was," he said. "This is different. This is real.

So say yes."

104

Day Four
July 18
Friday Morning

The man bent down, grabbed Yardley's face and started to pull her to her feet. She kicked with her right leg with all her might and landed a foot directly to his crotch. He shouted something incoherently and dropped to the ground.

Yardley ran but a hand grabbed her ankle and pulled her down.

She pulled at her bonds.

Her hands wouldn't loosen.

Not an inch.

The man still had her by the leg but was curling up into a ball. Yardley got behind him with her back to his, then swung her hands around his neck and arched her back as tight as she could.

The rope dug into his throat.

He twisted and rolled violently.

The pain in Yardley's shoulders was unbearable.

She didn't care.

She pulled and pulled and pulled.

It took a long time before the man stopped moving.

Five or six minutes.

Maybe longer.

When it was over, she got herself loose from the entanglement, muscled to her feet and walked back to the hole. The knife wasn't there so she had to open the car door and rub the ropes on the edge of the metal for a long time before breaking free.

She reburied the scroll and placed the moss rock back on top.

Then she dragged the man's body out of the field, to the road and put him in the trunk.

She drove out of the service road and headed away from the city.

The flatlands gave way to rolling hills, which then gave way to foothills. Half an hour later, she turned onto a dirt road that wound into ponderosa pines. She dragged the body as far as she could, which must have been a good three hundred yards. Then she got back in the car, headed for the city and abandoned it three miles from her house.

Walking the rest of the way, she had one thought and one thought only, namely that the only person in the world who knew Taylor Lee's whereabouts was dead.

Taylor was in the process of rotting to death.

That was last night.

Now it was morning.

She got dressed, headed to Larimer Street and knocked on the office door of a man she didn't personally know but who was reputed to be the best private investigator in Denver.

A man named Bryson Wilde.

No one answered.

She tried the knob.

It was locked.

She knocked again, "Anyone home?"

Silence.

She left and headed down the street for breakfast. When she returned, the door was unlocked. She stuck her head inside and saw a man making coffee. He had a solid physique, evident even under a grey suit, with black wingtips down below and thick blond hair up top, combed straight back. His eyes were green. His face was tanned and belonged on the cover of a magazine.

"Are you Bryson Wilde?"

"Yes."

"I really hope you can help me," she said. "I have something desperate going on."

Wilde looked like he was about to turn her away.

Instead he said, "Do you want some coffee?"

Yes.

She did.

She couldn't pay him up front.

She'd have to save up.

He didn't care.

He was more interested in the coffee.

She was just about to explain the situation when she had a question. "If I tell you things, do you keep them confidential?"

Yes.

He did.

"How do I know?"

He shrugged.

"You know because I just told you," he said. "What's on

your mind?"

She exhaled.

"A friend of mine was abducted," she said. "She was taken to a dark place and handcuffed. A man was keeping her there; he was doing it to force me to do something. I ended up killing him. That's why I'm coming to you instead of the police. It was mostly self-defense, but I'm a lawyer and really don't want it on my record."

"You're a lawyer?"

She nodded.

"What's your name?"

"Yardley Savannah," she said. "I need you to find her before she dies. I figure you can do that as well as the police."

Wilde lit a pack of matches and studied her through the flames.

"What's your friend's name?"

"Taylor Lee." She pulled a photo from her purse and pushed it across the desk. "That's her."

105

Day Four
July 18
Friday Morning

Wilde expected the photo to show the face of a stranger. The woman was familiar. He'd seen her somewhere before.

"She's pretty," he said.

"Yes."

Pretty was actually too light a word. Men would crawl through a field of broken glass just to smell her neck, that's the kind of woman she was.

Shinny brown hair, styled with bangs like Betty Page.

Lips as hot as Havana asphalt.

Green eyes.

Mid-twenties.

Expensive on every level.

Suddenly he realized who it was.

She was Neva—the woman who saw Night Neveraux leaving Grace Somerfield's house Saturday night. She was Wilde's client, with brown hair now instead of strawberry. He must have had a look on his face because Yardley asked, "Is everything okay?"

He cocked his head.

"Is her name Neva?"

"No, it's Taylor, Taylor Lee."

"Does she go by the nickname Neva?"

"No, why?"

Wilde almost blurted out, *She's a client of mine. She told me her name was Neva.* He also remembered promising her 100 percent confidentiality.

"Sorry," he said. "She looks like someone I know. So, her name's Taylor Lee."

"Right."

"Tell me everything you know about where she was being kept."

The woman recanted that she was taken to the place last night and wore a blindfold the whole time, which wasn't taken off until she was inside.

"Describe the inside."

Yardley wrinkled her face.

"It was pitch-black," she said. "He shined a flashlight on Taylor. That's all I really remember seeing, her face lit up with that flashlight. It was so eerie and surreal."

"What else do you remember?"

"Nothing."

"Think."

She did, then shook her head.

"Nothing."

Wilde pressed her for details, asking specific questions— how far the drive was, whether it was straight or twisty, wheth- er she heard other cars, how far was it from the trunk of the car to where Taylor was being held, whether she heard any animals or people or cars or sounds, et cetera.

She remembered a few things but not many.

"Let me think about it."

"Her time's running out."

"I understand. Give me a number where I can call you later."

She did.

Then left.

From the window, Wilde watched her walk down Larimer Street and disappear around a corner.

He was positive that Taylor Lee and Neva were the same person. Maybe Neva was wearing a strawberry wig when she came to see him. Maybe she was an actual strawberry at that moment and dyed it brunette afterwards.

He didn't know.

It didn't matter.

The two women were the same, that's what mattered.

Neva said she was a lesbian.

Was Yardley Savannah her lover?

Was she the one Neva was trying to protect?

Suddenly the door opened. Alabama busted in, ran to the rack, grabbed Wilde's hat and tossed it to him.

"Come on, we got to get out of here."

"Where have you—"

"Not now," she said. "There's an arrest warrant out on Night Neveraux for the murder of Grace Somerfield. There's another one out on you for aiding and abetting her after the fact."

"Raven."

"Right, Raven," Alabama said. "Hurry up."

Wilde grabbed his gun and a handful of matchbooks, then

put his hat on. They ran down the hall towards the back of the building as heavy footsteps came up the stairs from the street.

106

Day Four
July 18
Friday Morning

Ying took Danton downstairs and retrieved a cylindrical tube from behind a stack of boxes under the stairs. She carefully pulled out an old canvas and gently unrolled it on a wooden bench. It was clearly in Renoir style and had an ancient aura to it.

"How do you know it's original?" Danton asked.

"Jessica Dent authenticated it."

Danton raised an eyebrow.

"How'd she do that?"

"That's what she did," Ying said. "She had degrees in both art and history, neither of which were worth much until she met a woman in the black market."

"How'd you get a hold of it?"

She shrugged.

"Jessica was the cautious type," she said. "She had it in her possession to authenticate and appraise it. It was an important piece and she was nervous having it at her place. On occasion, she'd used me and another friend—a woman named

Constance Black—to hold onto things for her. I happened to have it at my house when she got taken by that madman and ended up getting her stomached carved on."

Danton pictured it and shook his head.

"You said before you thought a cop did that to her," he said.

"Right."

"You told me the name of the guy in charge."

"Warner Raven."

Right.

Warner Raven.

Danton scratched his head.

"Who gave Jessica the painting to authenticate?"

"I don't know."

"He never came looking for it?"

"I'm sure he did," Ying said. "He didn't know anything about me, though."

"Interesting."

Danton wrinkled his face.

"Maybe Raven's the one who gave it to her," Danton said.

Ying laughed.

"He couldn't afford a painting like this," she said.

"Maybe he didn't buy it."

"What do you mean?"

"Well, Raven's a homicide detective," Danton said. "Maybe he stumbled across it when he searched a house—maybe a victim's house, or maybe even a suspect's house. Maybe he decided to stick it in the trunk of his car when no one was looking."

Ying tilted her head.

"That's actually possible."

"Play it out," Danton said. "He has the painting but isn't sure if it's real or how much it's worth. Somehow, he learns that Jessica's in the business. He gives it to her for review. She tells him it's authentic but is still working on how much it's worth. In the meantime, she gives it to you."

"Okay, go on."

"Now that he knows it's authentic, he begins to worry about Jessica being a loose end, a loose end that lives in the same town as him, to be exact," he said. "He gets visions of her blackmailing him down the road. So he kills her and makes it look like a madman did it, someone from his past. The only problem is, when he goes to her place to get the painting back, it's gone."

"Wow."

"Right, wow."

107

Day Four
July 18
Friday Morning

Yardley was at her office when the phone rang and a voice that she never expected to hear again came through, the voice of Blanche Twister, the university professor.

"I had a strange thought last night," she said.

Yardley didn't care.

She was still half convinced that Twister was the woman in the cab, the person pulling the strings of the first "client" who tried to trick her into giving up the scroll.

"Look—"

"Just hear me out," Twister said. "The scroll you have doesn't identify the starting points. We talked about the possibility that maybe there was a second scroll, one that had only the starting points but nothing else. In effect, you had to have both scrolls to locate the treasures."

Right.

Yardley remembered the theory.

"'I've come up with another thought," Twister said. "Maybe

there is no second scroll. Maybe the starting points were very prominent landmarks at the time. Maybe they were the kind of things that couldn't be forgotten."

Yardley exhaled.

"Like what?"

"Well, at that point in history, there were a number of temples, forts and pyramids along the northern Nile," Twister said. "Maybe they were used as the starting points. Maybe the first five prominent structures that they came to, they used the western most point of the structure, or something like that, as the starting point."

Yardley ran her fingers through her hair.

She didn't care right now.

Her thoughts were on Taylor, who was somewhere in a dark place dying.

"Maybe," she said.

"Well, I just thought I'd mention it."

"Yeah, thanks."

"I wasn't the woman in the cab," Twister added.

"Okay."

108

Day Four
July 18
Friday Morning

F riday.

This was it.

This was the day Nicole would die.

To be even more exact, this was the day Nicole would die at the hands of Warner Raven. It was also the day she'd get words carved into her stomach. Wilde was ninety-five percent sure of Raven's guilt last night. The arrest warrant this morning brought his certainty up to a hundred. It was nothing more than a vehicle to get Wilde off the streets even though, technically, it was justified.

Alabama's story about last night further confirmed it.

She hid on the floorboard in the back seat of Raven's car, taking every perceivable caution to not get spotted by Raven or his strange night partner, Johnny Pants, which wasn't easy given that there was almost no talking. They ended up in a pitch-black railroad yard northwest of the city. There the men got out and slipped into the darkness. Alabama tried to follow but got separated. After an hour, she got the hell out of there and spent a long time walking before she came to a public phone where she could call a cab. When she got back to Wilde's place, he wasn't home. She got up at sunrise, left a note on the refrigerator door, and then headed to the office to see if he was there.

He wasn't.

She went out for breakfast.

When she came back, he was there.

Now they were on the run. They rented a car in Alabama's name and headed for the railroad yard Alabama got driven to last night. "Nicole's there somewhere," Wilde said. "After I confirm it, I'm going to kill Raven with my bare hands. Same thing for his little asshole partner, Johnny Pants."

"I wonder what Pants' role is in all this."

"I don't know but he's definitely in it throat deep," Wilde said. "They'll come for Nicole tonight. I'll be waiting for them."

"Carve something in Raven's stomach," Alabama said. "Make it look like the madman did it."

Wilde nodded.

Good idea.

Very good idea.

They were heading farther and farther out of the city.

Wilde told Alabama about the visit from Yardley Savannah this morning, including the fact that her missing friend, Taylor Lee, was actually Neva.

"I don't get what's going on," he said.

"Something."

"You've got that right." A beat then, "Now that you got me thinking about this railroad yard, I'm starting to wonder if Taylor Lee is being kept in a boxcar."

"You think?"

He shrugged.

"It's possible," he said. "Yardley got thrust over the guy's shoulders for a short climb up some stairs or a ladder before they entered the room where Taylor was being held. A boxcar would have a ladder. Also, Yardley remembered the sound of a rolling steel door."

Alabama wrinkled her forehead.

"You're thinking," Wilde said.

Yes.

She was.

"I don't think you should kill Raven," she said.

"Why not?"

"Once you get that dirty, there's no way to ever get clean again."

Wilde wasn't impressed.

"I've killed before."

"That was the war," Alabama said. "This is different."

"Is it?"

109

Day Four
July 18
Friday Morning

The railroad yard was a graveyard of decommissioned gondolas, flatbeds and boxcars waiting to be parted out or cut for scrap. Most of the cars—there were hundreds of them—looked to be thirty, forty or fifty years old, long past their useful lives.

Rust was the name of the game.

Wilde's heart raced.

"Nicole's here somewhere."

They made a quick pass on foot up and down the rails, calling out Nicole's name but getting no response. The sun beat down. The heavy yard metal and gravel soaked it up and shot it straight into Wilde's pores.

"Hot," he said, wiping his forehead.

Alabama grunted.

They started at the far end and began to go through the cars one at a time. Lots of the doors were rusted shut and had to be pried open with a crowbar.

One after another, they searched.

So far there was no Nicole, no smell of fresh urine, no spent food containers or other signs that someone had been held in captivity.

Wilde's hands were covered with rust and grease.

An unhealthy portion of that had migrated to his face.

He'd never been so dirty or sweaty.

His suit was ruined.

Pigeon droppings were everywhere.

So were mice, rats and lizards.

"Keep a lookout for rattlesnakes," he told Alabama.

Hour after hour, they searched.

Then they ran out of cars.

Wilde sat down on the shady side of a gondola and leaned against the wheel.

"She's got to be here," he said. "How did we miss her?"

Alabama sat next to him.

"We didn't miss her. She's not here."

"Then what was Raven doing here last night?"

"I don't know. Maybe he was just scoping the place out to move her here tonight."

Wilde bowed his head in his hand.

"I'd give everything I own for a glass of ice water. We should have stopped somewhere and got supplies."

"We didn't know it would take this long."

True, but still—

He looked to the left and spotted a solitary boxcar off by itself, three or four hundred yards down a side rail. It looked slightly crooked as if it had derailed and then got abandoned in place.

He stood up. "Come on. One more."

Alabama frowned at how far it was.

"You got to be kidding."

He headed that way.

"If I was going to stash Nicole somewhere, that's where I'd do it."

When they got there, Wilde saw something interesting, namely a fresh padlock on the door.

He shot it off.

Muffled sounds came from inside.

Wilde slid the door open.

Inside he found Taylor Lee slumped on the floor with her wrists handcuffed over her head. He pulled a gag out of her mouth and she gasped for air.

She had no food or water.

The temperature had to be a hundred and ten.

She was alive but not by much.

Alabama hugged her and told her she was safe now while Wilde inspected the handcuffs. "I'm going to have to shoot these off," he said. "We'll get a ricochet and not necessarily a good one. Alabama, you wait outside."

"No."

Alabama covered the woman's body with hers and said, "Do it."

Wilde held his breath, put the end of the barrel against the chain of the cuffs and said, "Everyone ready?"

Yes.

"On three," he said.

Then he counted.

One, two, three!

Bam!

Alabama screamed.

110

Day Four
July 18
Friday Night

Friday night after dark a heavy rain fell out of a black sky. Rain wasn't the right word, storm was more like it. Thunderstorm was even more like it. Yardley sat on the fire escape hunched against the building in the dry spot, sipping white wine from a bottle.

Her legs were stretched out.

The rain fell on her feet and shins.

The client was dead.

Taylor had been found.

Things could have turned out worse.

Lightning arced across the sky.

Fierce.

Violent.

Suddenly a figure crawled out of the window and sat next to her. It was Taylor.

"We knocked, you didn't answer," she said.

We?

A second figure joined them. It was a man, handsome,

about forty, wearing a brown suit and matching hat. Yardley recognized him as Everett Somerfield, Esq., a high-profile attorney and former husband of Grace Somerfield who was murdered last Saturday.

Taylor introduced him.

"This is a surprise," Yardley said.

Taylor put an arm around Yardley's shoulders and squeezed. "Thanks again for hiring Wilde to find me. The only reason I'm alive is because of you."

Yardley shrugged.

"No problem."

Taylor's face grew serious. "We have a few things to tell you," she said. "I'm not necessarily proud of what I'm going to tell you. Let me say that right off the bat."

Things?

What things?

"Everett and I have been together for some time," she said.

Everett nodded.

"We fell in love a year ago, while I was still married to Grace. Neither of us planned it. It was just one of those things that happen."

Taylor put her hand on the wine bottle and said, "You feel like sharing?"

Sure.

No problem.

Taylor took a long swig, followed by Everett, then back to Taylor.

"Okay, here comes the bad part," Taylor said.

"We needed money and decided to take some from Grace," she said. "Everett knew what she had and where she kept it, namely in the safe in the master bedroom. He also knew the combination. Grace usually has a board meeting at the museum on Saturday nights. Last Saturday, Everett made himself visible downtown—getting a public alibi in effect—while I broke into Grace's place."

Yardley blurted out the question on her mind.

"You're the one who killed her?"

Taylor answered without hesitation.

"No."

"No?"

"No."

She took another swig of wine.

"I got the safe open, took everything out, put it in a pillowcase that I'd brought and closed it back up," she said. "I was on my way out when Grace suddenly came home out of the blue. I was trapped and ducked into the next room. She fiddled around downstairs for five or ten minutes then came up to the bedroom and started to get ready for bed. I just stayed quiet, waiting for her to get into bed and fall asleep. Then something unexpected happened. A woman showed up. I saw her sneaking up the stairs with a knife in her hand. She was blond and had her hair up. There was a tattoo behind her ear."

"Night Neveraux," Yardley said.

Taylor nodded.

"Right, Night Neveraux, although I didn't know her name at the time. She went into the bedroom and said, *I want the scroll.* Grace said, *What scroll?* The woman—Night—said, *Don't play dumb—the scroll Emmanuelle gave you for safekeeping.* Grace hesitated then said, *It's in the safe.* Night said, *Open it.* That's when I snuck down the stairs and left."

Lightning flashed.

Close.

A deafening clap of thunder exploded overhead.

Yardley jumped.

"Close," Taylor said.

"Anyway, I waited outside across the street to see if I could get any information on this woman after she came out," Taylor said. "She eventually appeared and headed for a car. I snuck over in the shadows until I was close enough to get the license plate number. It was FC211. She squealed out of there."

"Okay."

"Me and Everett met up later," Taylor said. "I had the scroll, of course, along with Grace's jewels. We didn't know anything about the scroll at the time other than a suspicion that it was worth a fortune."

"That's correct," Everett said.

"Monday, I read in the paper that Grace had been murdered Saturday night," Taylor said. "That's when I got scared."

111

Day Four
July 18
Friday Night

W hen I read that Grace had been murdered, the last thing I wanted was to be caught with the things from her safe in my possession," Taylor said. "Stealing is one thing. Being implicated in a murder is something else. Everett and I came up with a plan. We traced the license plate number FC211 to a woman named Night Neveraux. Since we knew that she was the one who killed Grace, we decided to plant the stuff at her house. We did that Monday night, we hid the stuff in one of her shoeboxes in the closet."

"Wow."

Right.

Wow.

"The more we thought about Night killing Grace, the more we decided that she needed to be brought to justice," Taylor said. "On Tuesday morning, I put on a strawberry wig and went to the office of a private investigator named Bryson Wilde."

"My Bryson Wilde?" Yardley said.

Right.

Him.

"I told him I was making love to a woman in a car Saturday night and saw someone run out of Grace Somerfield's yard. It was so strange that I got the woman's license plate number, which was FC211. I later found out Grace was dead. I wanted Wilde to make a substitute police report on my behalf. That way, I'd stay out of the picture while bringing Night to justice." A beat. "Wilde fell for it and made the call. When the police searched Night's place, they didn't find the stuff from the safe that I'd planted there. I don't know why. Anyway, that's neither here nor there. It's really not important. What's important is that I kept the scroll."

"You did?"

Taylor nodded.

"Then I did something I shouldn't have," she said. "I didn't know if anyone knew that Grace was holding the scroll for this Emmanuelle woman that Night referred to. To play it safe, though, just in case the scroll could be traced back to Grace, I decided to distance myself from it. I hired a man to have it delivered to our table as we ate lunch. I made it a delivery from a vague client, which could have been yours or could have been mine. My plan was for you to take the scroll as a temporary measure. If it ever got traced back to Grace, both you and me could back each other up in that it was mysteriously delivered to our table. The mystery client would be the suspect, not you or me."

Yardley tensed.

"You set me up."

Taylor exhaled.

"Not really," she said. "You were never in any danger. What

happened next is what I didn't expect. I thought you would just keep the scroll safe and leave it alone. Instead, you started to investigate it. You went to that professor, Blanche Twister, and told her about it. Then she started to get interested in it and—as far as I can tell—hired someone to pretend to be your client, in an effort to trick you into giving her the scroll. The woman you saw in the cab wasn't me. It had to have been her."

"Is that the truth?"

"It is, it's the absolute truth," Taylor said. "Anyway, now I was worried about someone trying to get the scroll out of your hands. I needed to get it back without letting you catch on to any of the background. Unfortunately, it had a hold on you."

True.

Very true.

"You pretended that someone had taken it but I knew in my heart that you still had it," Taylor said. "The fake client idea that Twister used on you was a good one, so good that I adopted it. Me and Everett hired a friend of his—a man named Paul Slipstone—to pretend to be my client. He told you he'd kill me if you didn't get the scroll to him by noon. I thought that would be good enough to pry it loose from you. It wasn't."

No.

It wasn't.

"That forced us to take things to the next level," Taylor said. "We scouted around and found an old boxcar. I vanished at lunchtime and never returned, as if I'd been abducted. The client then took you to me that night. All the time, I was just waiting there. When he pulled up in the car, I put the handcuffs on and stuck a gag in my mouth. I had to make it look realistic. The plan was for him to make you get the scroll, then he'd come back and release me. Unfortunately, you killed him."

Everett motioned for the wine bottle.

Yardley handed it to him.

He took a long swallow and said, "That brings us to now. The way I see it, we've put you through enough trauma that you're entitled to be a joint partner in the scroll. We're each entitled to one-third of it."

He stopped talking.

Both of them looked at Yardley, waiting for her reaction.

"I have no problem with that," she said.

That was true, too.

"So where is it?"

Yardley paused.

Then she said, "It's buried out by some railroad tracks."

"Let's go get it."

"Right now?"

Yes.

Right now.

"Why now?"

"Because it has a hold on you," Everett said. "Let's get it over with while we all agree as to what's right. We'll get it, keep it here at your place for the night and then decide tomorrow what to do with it."

Lightning flashed.

Yardley stood up.

The wine made her legs wobble.

"Okay," she said. "Let's go."

112

Day Four
July 18
Friday Night

A drizzle started at sunset and got heavier and heavier as night rolled in. In the shadows of that storm, Wilde approached Raven's house with a dark heart.

This was it.

Friday night.

Game time.

With a hammer and screwdriver, he punched out the trunk lock of Raven's car and pulled the lid up. Then he pounded on the inside latch until it broke off. He pulled the spare tire out and rolled it behind the hedges. Then he tossed the tools into the neighbor's yard, climbed in the trunk, pulled the lid closed and cinched it down with a belt.

There.

He was in.

Wherever Raven went, he'd be with him.

He waited.

Nothing happened.

Minute after claustrophobic minute passed.

Wilde almost got out a hundred times but forced himself not to.

His breathing got heavy.

The oxygen was getting thin.

Then it happened.

Raven got in, fired up the engine and squealed out of the driveway. The vehicle stayed in motion for ten or fifteen minutes and stopped. Raven got out but left the engine running.

What was he doing?

Suddenly a payphone rang.

Raven said, "It's me." Moments passed without further talking from his end. Then he said, "Okay," hopped back in the vehicle and took off.

Wilde wiped sweat off his forehead.

He already had the gun out of his waistband.

He twisted it in his fingers in the dark.

Traffic sounds got lighter and lighter. They were heading out of the city. Then the asphalt gave way to gravel, which further gave way to dirt.

They were somewhere remote.

Suddenly the vehicle stopped.

Raven sat there, not getting out.

What was he doing?

Then he got out and shut the door.

Wilde got on his back and pointed the gun up, just in case Raven was coming into the trunk. That didn't happen. He released the belt and raised the lid. The storm immediately pounded on him, cold and invasive.

The night was thick.

Wilde got out and looked around.

He saw nothing.

The world was blacker than black.

Suddenly lightning arced across the sky.

It lit up the warehouse district. Raven was parked in front of the large building, the one with blood on the concrete, the one with the shed out back where Jessica Dent had been kept, the one Wilde had checked twice to no avail.

Raven was climbing in the side window.

Wilde ran that way.

His footsteps were inaudible.

The heavy pounding of the storm masked them.

Hold on, Nicole.

Just a few more minutes.

He got through the window and was surprised at how quiet everything suddenly got. The splash of a flashlight came from the stairwell.

Wilde headed that way.

The light continued up, all the way to the top floor.

Close the gap.

Close the gap.

Close the gap.

He sped up, now only ten or fifteen steps behind, as Raven walked through the door into the top floor. The door shut behind him and the flashlight disappeared. Wilde raced up the stairs two at a time and opened the door enough to stick his head in.

The flashlight came back into view.

It was pointed at a woman.

Nicole.

She was roped against the wall in a standing, spread-eagle position.

She wore pants but her blouse and bra were gone.

Her eyes were blindfolded.

A gag filled her mouth.

She pulled at her bonds as Raven ran the light down her body and then back up.

Wilde trained the gun at the man's back and tightened his finger on the trigger.

See you in hell, asshole!

113

Day Four
July 18
Friday Night

Yardley didn't say much other than give directions as they drove through the storm to the railroad tracks. The windshield wipers beat back and forth with full power but were still losing the battle. No other cars were on the road. All the sane people in the world were home watching TV or sleeping.

They got to the service road and stopped.

No headlights were in front of them.

None were behind.

"Looks clear," Taylor said.

They headed down the road, which was muddy but not impassable. The bodies of Michael Spencer and Kent Dawson came into view on their left, snuggled into the recesses of a grouping of rabbit brush.

Everett studied the bodies but didn't slow down.

"Is that Slipstone?"

"No," Yardley said.

"It's not? Who is it?"

"I don't know," she said. "They just showed up here."

"Weird."

"This road is cursed."

The headlights punched into a pinion pine and Yardley said, "Pull over by that tree. The scroll's buried out in the field under a rock."

They stopped and killed the lights and engine.

"We should have brought a flashlight," Taylor said.

Yardley pulled one out of her purse.

"I did."

She led them into the field and sprayed the light on the rock. "It's under that rock," she said. "About a foot down."

Everett grunted.

"I suppose I get the honors."

"Looks that way."

Yardley handed the flashlight to Taylor and said, "I'll be right back."

"Where you going?"

"To get rid of a little wine."

She took twenty steps, relieved herself and came back just as Everett was pulling the scroll out of the ground. He took it out of the pillowcase and held it out for the rain to wash off a layer of dirt.

"It looks like it's in good shape."

Taylor trained the light on it.

"It looks perfect. I was worried."

Everett handed it to her and she took a closer look with the light. When Yardley looked back at the man, he had a gun in his hand.

It was pointed at her.

"Thanks for bringing us here," he said.

"Everett, don't," Taylor said.

"Got to," he said. Then to Yardley, "I'm sorry to say this, but your piece of the partnership has just been cancelled." Then he looked at Taylor and said, "Yours too."

"Everett!"

"Sorry," he said.

"You bastard."

He trained the barrel at Yardley's heart.

She froze.

So did Taylor.

Then he pulled the trigger.

114

Day Four
July 18
Friday Night

Wilde's finger tightened on the trigger but he couldn't plant the bullet in the man's back. Do it as soon as he turns. A heartbeat later Raven started to turn. In less than a second Wilde would have the shot.

"You're right on time."

The words were like fire in Wilde's veins, not because of their meaning, but because they didn't come from Raven's mouth. They came from someone else, another man somewhere in the room. They startled Raven as much as they did Wilde judging by the way he swung the flashlight at them.

A man lit up.

A strong man.

In his hand was a gun pointed at Raven's chest.

"I don't know who you are," Raven said, "but whatever is going on is between you and me. Let the woman go."

"Let the woman go?"

The words were laced with mockery.

"That's what you want me to do? Let her go?"

"You got me," Raven said. "I'm unarmed. I followed your instructions. Just do what you're going to do to me and get it over with."

A gun fired.

The flashlight in Raven's hand exploded and went out with a blue flash. The man with the gun turned on his own flashlight and shined it into Raven's face. "That's better," he said. "Now I'm more comfortable. My name's Degare Danton. You don't know me. You never knew me. You never will know me."

Raven held his hands up in defense.

"I don't understand what's going on."

"That's because you're stupid," Danton said.

"Enlighten me."

Danton laughed.

Then he got serious and said, "Sure, why not. I guess you deserve that much before you die. There was a woman named Jessica Dent. I gave her a painting to authenticate. She didn't give it back. She said someone stole it from her. That was a lie. She needed to die."

"I don't understand."

"When you're in my business you learn how to cover your tracks," Danton said. "I called you and said you'd die on Friday. You didn't follow directions. You tried to catch me. I knew you'd do that. Then I killed Jessica Dent and carved those words in her stomach. You remember those words, don't you?"

"Yes."

"I thought you might," Danton said. "That was all a ruse. The intent was to make you and everyone else in the world think that the killer was someone you knew, someone from your past, someone who had a grudge against you. In short, someone who wasn't me. See what I mean when I said you were stupid?"

Raven shifted his feet.

"Just let the woman go."

"You say that as if she's some kind of innocent little thing," Danton said. "Do you want to know something about her? She's a hit woman. She came here to Denver to kill me and a woman named Emmanuelle. She was hired by a Greek man named Javin Petracca. Do you know why he hired her?"

Raven said nothing.

"What's wrong, don't you like my little story?" Danton said. "He hired her because me and Emmanuelle stole something from him, a golden scroll to be precise. In the process, his wife—a little flower named Alexia—got shot. It was an accident but Petracca's not an understanding man. He's a vengeful one."

"Good for him."

Danton smiled.

"You have some balls, I'll hand you that." He flashed the light on Nicole and said, "Getting back to your innocent little friend there, she found Emmanuelle yesterday and killed her. Did you know that? No, you probably didn't. So, do you still want her to go free?"

"You're lying."

"Pull the gag out of her mouth and ask her," Danton said.

Raven complied.

"It's true," the woman said.

"See?" Danton said. "You're probably wondering what she's doing in Denver. The reason she's here is because Emmanuelle, bless her heart, double-crossed me after we stole the scroll. She took it and then tried to kill me. That didn't work. Then she brought it to Denver and gave it to an old friend of hers for safekeeping until the dust cleared. That old friend is named Grace Somerfield." A beat then, "That's a nice expression you have on your face. You've been trying to find her killer. Well, guess what? You just found him. I'm the one who killed her. Saturday night. All I wanted was the scroll. I gave her a chance to give it to me. She said someone stole it. That's the same kind of bullshit that Jessica Dent tried to pull on me. I wasn't in the mood for it and slit her throat. That pisses you off, doesn't it?"

"You little bastard."

"That's good," Danton said. "Anger is good. The reason I'm telling you all of this is to get you mad. You're getting there, aren't you? Let me know when you're as pissed as you can get, because when you are, I'm going to put this gun down and let you have your shot at me, man to man, bare fists to the death. So tell me, are you mad enough yet?"

"You're crazy."

Danton put the gun on the floor.

Then he laid the flashlight on a bench and said, "Come on and get me."

"You're nuts."

"You're afraid. Look at you, you're scared to death."

115

Day Four
July 18
Friday Night

Wilde stepped out of the shadows and said, "I'll take that offer." Danton froze and saw Wilde's gun trained on his face. He was trapped.

"Untie the woman," Wilde told Raven.

The man complied.

"Now give her your car keys."

He did but added, "She's a killer."

"Too bad."

"Helping her is a felony."

"Shut up."

Then to Nicole, "Go on and get out of here."

She ran.

"Now sit on the floor, both of you. We're all going to hold tight for ten minutes while she gets a nice long head start."

"This is obstruction of justice," Raven said.

"Shut up."

They waited without talking.

No one said a word.

Wilde suddenly realized why Raven had been snooping around at night, he wasn't hiding a woman, he was looking for the killer's lair.

Ten minutes passed.

Good enough.

"Both of you get back against the wall."

When they did, Wilde went over to Danton's gun and picked it up off the floor. He emptied the chambers and threw the bullets into the darkness. They landed with a metallic ping and rolled.

"Get out of here," he told Raven. "Don't go after Nicole. Do you understand? Not tonight, not ever."

A long hesitation.

Raven said nothing.

Then he walked briskly towards the stairwell.

116

Day Four
July 18
Friday Night

When Everett pulled the trigger the hammer came down with a solid click but a bullet didn't fire. He kept the weapon trained on Yardley's heart and pulled again.

Click.

Click.

Click.

Suddenly a shot fired but it didn't come from Everett, it came from Taylor. Everett grabbed his chest and dropped to the ground. He twitched while horrible sounds escaped from his mouth. Then he got deathly silent and stopped moving.

Taylor dropped her weapon to the ground.

Her hands trembled.

Her eyes watered.

Her knees wobbled and then buckled.

Yardley grabbed her and broke the fall before she hit the ground. Then she wrapped her arms around the woman and rocked her.

"It's okay," she said. "Everything's okay."

The storm beat down.

It was cold.

Invasive.

"I thought he might try something like that," Taylor said.

They didn't get up for a long time.

Maybe five minutes.

Maybe ten.

Then they got to their feet, left the body where it was, picked up the scroll and headed for the car.

117

Day Four
July 18
Friday Night

Wilde kept his weapon trained on Danton long enough for Raven to get out of the building. Then he emptied the bullets from his gun and threw them into the darkness. He tossed the gun in the opposite direction of the bullets and walked into the middle of the room.

"Come on."

Danton immediately charged.

His face was distorted.

Insane.

Hardened with hate.

Wilde balled his fist and connected a violent punch to Danton's face, so hard that the man's head snapped back and took him to the ground.

He shook for a moment then stopped moving.

No breathing came from his chest.

No twitching came from his limbs.

His eyes were open, unblinking, staring at nothing.

Wilde stood over him with clenched fists and let out a

blood-curdling yell.

Get up!

Get up!

Get up!

The man didn't get up.

He didn't move an inch.

Wilde waited heartbeat after pounding heartbeat as the frantic air rushing in and out of his lungs slowly got back to normal. Then he slumped down on the floor next to the man and stared at his face.

Alabama was right.

He'd never be clean again.

He closed the man's eyelids and staggered towards the stairwell.

Suddenly something happened he didn't expect. Heavy footsteps pounded up the stairs, moving at a dangerous speed in the pitch-black darkness.

He shined the flashlight.

A body swung around the landing into view.

It was Nicole.

He bounded down to meet her and held her tighter than tight.

She buried her face in his chest and cried. Then she said, "I didn't kill Emmanuelle."

"I don't care."

"Danton did," she said. "Come to Paris with me."

About the Author

Formerly a longstanding trial attorney before taking the big leap and devoting his fulltime attention to writing, RJ Jagger (that's a penname, by the way) is the author of over twenty hard-edged mystery and suspense thrillers. In addition to his own books, Jagger also ghostwrites for a well-known, bestselling author. He is a member of the International Thriller Writers and the Mystery Writers of America.

RJJAGGER.com